BEST MICROFICTION

2022

Series Editors

Meg Pokrass, Gary Fincke

Guest Editor

Tania Hershman

BEST MICROFICTION 2022
ISBN 978-1-949790-61-0
eISBN 978-1-949790-62-7

First Pelekinesis Printing 2022

For information:

Pelekinesis
112 Harvard Ave #65
Claremont, CA 91711 USA

ISSN 2641-9750

Best Microfiction 2022

Best Microfiction Anthology Series

Series Editors
Meg Pokrass, Gary Fincke

Guest Editor
Tania Hershman

Social Media Director
Travis Guzman

Production Editor
Cooper Renner

Copy Editor
Michelle Christophorou

Interviews
Audra Kerr Brown

Editorial Assistant/Scouts
April Bradley, Melissa Llanes Brownlee

Layout and Design
Mark Givens

Cover illustration
Terry M. Givens

TABLE OF CONTENTS

BEST MICROFICTION

INTERVIEWS

THREE ESSAYS ON THE CRAFT OF MICROFICTION BY PEOPLE WHO KNOW WHAT THEY'RE TALKING ABOUT

FOREWORD

MEG POKRASS AND GARY FINCKE,
SERIES CO-EDITORS

Selecting a winning story is akin to falling in love. When editing and selecting for a yearly anthology, it comes down to something like finding a mysterious connection to a particular story. We read and reread these wonderful stories, so impressed with the editorial nominations from the literary magazines who are bringing this form into the light. Each year, we find that screening and reading hundreds and hundreds of micros to be an exciting but difficult challenge given the plethora of increasingly strong nominations.

Once again this year the majority of micros were original, insightful, and entertaining. We found the variety of approaches fascinating. There were stories that showed the reader everything and yet made us gasp in surprise, and other stories that gave away nothing, but worked on the reader through every invisible word, through precisely *what was not told.* Some characters were lightly sketched, and others created in microscopic detail. There were recurring themes; many this year involving the death of our planet as climate change continues to haunt our waking hours, as well as stories about violence against those who are most vulnerable.

Structurally, many of these tiny beauties held us in their grip all the way through, but lost us as late as the final sentence. Endings are excruciatingly hard to master, and yet they remain the key to success in this form. Universally speaking, with a word-count so small, the story intensity must be proportionately large. As readers, we prefer to feel as if we're uncovering the larger meaning. We like to be trusted.

Best Microfiction, now four years old, has become the diverse, international anthology series we agreed we wanted to create nearly five years ago. It's been a shared pleasure for us to read the submissions of editors from literary journals located on multiple continents. Moreover, we have been fortunate to have worked with four guest editors—Dan Chaon, Michael Martone, Amber Sparks, and now Tania Hershman—all of whom have selected a full spectrum of voices, forms, and aesthetics across the nearly one hundred stories to be reprinted on these pages.

Introducing the newest volume of Best Microfiction is an excellent time to consider its evolution. Now well-established, our anthology demonstrates that it continues to change as it grows rather than being dedicated to a particular type of writing or a selection based on precedent. What has become our passion is to sustain a focus on selections from small, online journals. These magazines, nearly always labors of love, are to be celebrated for their quirky brilliance. Every year our guest editor has the opportunity to create an eclectic selection enriched with their personal sense of what resonates and makes them excited about the possibilities of the form. This year, readers will see that *Best Microfiction 2022*'s guest editor, Tania Hershman, continues the tradition of choosing beautiful, odd, haunting and original works.

INTRODUCTION

TANIA HERSHMAN, GUEST EDITOR

What a privilege it is to be asked to select the year's best microfictions, and what a pleasure to read several hundred of those that editors selected to represent their publications for the past year. I have a particular love for the shortest of short fiction. I love writing it—it was where my own writing career started, and whatever I also write now, poems, hybrids, longer fictions, I come back again and again to short short stories. And there's little I enjoy reading more than a gloriously written tiny story that is not excellent *in spite* of its length constraint, it embraces its brevity and uses it to make the story even more powerful.

A micro story doesn't have to be anything... except short. That's it, no genre requirements, no stylistic dictates. It has a certain number of words it needs to fall below, and apart from that, a writer has complete freedom. I love seeing what so many different writers do in that space, the way they shape words on the page, how microfiction gives permission to leave so much out, but also allows for depth, for richness, often in great part because of those intentional gaps. I was surprised, for example, by the number of the writers who chose the very long sentence to convey their story, which I think a very short piece can be ideal for—the writer controls the pacing, tells us when to breathe, or when not to, and it can be incredibly effective.

Some of the stories I've chosen tell of a few moments in time, some of a whole life. Often, stories circle around families, relationships, which are obviously popular materials for fiction. I loved it when writers looked further, too, and I take particular delight in the strange and the magical, which I also think microfiction is well suited to.

Reading is subjective, judging is down to not just the particular judge, but how they feel on that particular day. I hope you enjoy my choices, and that you—as I did—find new favourite writers and new favourite lit mags from within these pages. I thank all the writers for having the courage to send their stories into the world, and the amazing editors of all the literary magazines championing great writing of every stripe and flavour. Long live the shortest of stories!

BEST MICROFICTION

OTHER SHIT RUMPELSTILTSKIN DID

ANGELA READMAN

Teach his soldiers to fly, DIY parachutes drifting off a bridge. Steal his sister's doll and ask what's wrong with it? Learn to pronounce his name, make R's sound less like W and S's less like snakes. Lay a palm on the speech therapist's belly, fluttering fingers a blinking star. Ask his mother if boys can have babies. Why not? Bury his sister's scissors, liberate the doll that gave her a dirty look, cradle the shaved head to his chest. Wish on a breastbone. Write to Santa for a brother, a deerhound, a goldfish to love. Ruin another jumper. Learn to spell his name. Burn his alphabet blocks, the letters never enough. Scribble lines on a blackboard. I must not... steal... drill holes in lips... stuff pudding, honey, bread into dolls, no matter how hungry they look. Invent a game called BAM! Plot the death for his father in a half-arsed fashion: stampeding cows, possessed ploughs, a fatal allergy to the silver stuff on scratch cards (preferably winners). Experiment with nicknames: Stilts, Skin. Join a band. Quit.

Get a tattoo. Date a woman who thought he'd be taller. Date another who calls him Rump. Babysit her son, buy a globe & spin it. Make Egg Fried Rice a geography lesson. Eat day-old prawn crackers with David Attenborough. Pick up the phone to show the kid where the geese go. Hang up on the guy who sounds like he knows. Attend the aquarium with a lady who thought he'd be skinnier. Learn about seahorses, unfasten his belt flashing the seahorse inked to his hip. Laugh at the joke the kid next door told in the park. Take the long way around avoiding the park altogether, facts about octopus and The Beatles shielded by mothers. Put the Lucky House on speed dial, fill out forms, ask about adoption prospects for guys living alone. Snap the world off its stand, push the globe under a sweater and stroke it in front of the mirror like a beachball, a melon baby kicking inside him, bursting to be born.

Angela Readman's stories have won the Costa Short Story Award, the Mslexia competition, the National Flash Fiction Day competition and the New Flash Fiction Review competition. Her second story collection *The Girls are Pretty Crocodiles* was published in 2022. Nine Arches are publishing her poetry collection *Bunny Girls* later this year.

SHE HAS LOST SOMETHING AGAIN

MELISSA LLANES BROWNLEE

She's prone to losing things. A shoe here. A ring there. Fish find them in their bellies. Trees grow roots around them. She has a whole lake full of treasure filled fish boxes. A whole forest floor embedded with her wayward shoes, lost when she decided it was best to run from the prince than stay for the party. So many princes. So many parties. If the princes only knew that they wouldn't need her dowry if they just went fishing in the lake instead of fishing for her with their mango breasts and betel lips compliments as if being compared to food or spices was appealing at all. She would gladly lose a million bangles sliding down her arms into the gaping mouths of fish than wait for a prince to catch her.

Melissa Llanes Brownlee, a native Hawaiian writer in Japan, has work in *Booth*, *Pleiades*, *The Citron Review*, *Milk Candy Review*, *Necessary Fiction*, *trampset*, *jmww*, *Superstition Review*, *SmokeLong Quarterly*, and *Best Small Fictions* 2021. Read *Hard Skin*, her short story collection with Juventud Press. She tweets @lumchanmfa. Talks story at www.melissallanesbrownlee.com.

ROMANCE IN THE LOWER AND UPPER ATMOSPHERE

FRANKIE MCMILLAN

Him

Me with my girl in the grass gazing up at what looks like pinpricks in the great blanket of sky. It's getting cold. "Well, have you had enough?"

Back inside, she goes around the house, lighting candles. I don't know what she's got against electricity. Swarms are drawn to the flame and there's an awful burning smell.

Later she tells me we're like identical stars but moving in opposite directions.

"That's just today," I say, "Just today you feel that way."

That whole lunar month we orbit each other. My naked eye observes all her comings and goings, all her little divergences. She dyes her hair pink. She takes up running. Each day she runs further and further. When she gets up to speeds of 100 kms an hour I know I've got trouble. When a bright light streaks across the sky, followed by a trail of hot gas something inside me breaks.

I climb the roof. I square my jaw. "Go on, shoot me. Shoot me, lady star."

Her

I don't go on about Pluto because lying beside me in the grass is my twin star who complains the grass is getting damp, it's the dew and, *have I had enough yet, have I had enough of being out here because inside could be a lot warmer* so we go inside and I light candles, white votive candles, one over there, one over there until the whole house glows but I can see he's worried about swarms coming in and he looks at the windows as if by looking at them I'll know what he wants me to do and then he starts on about electricity, how it saves lives, and I say it's not about saving anything but he keeps on about how we should support the electric companies, and he's like a dog with a bone, he won't let go until I'm forced to say that maybe he's right and he comes over and tells me I'm awfully pretty and he leans over and blows on my face and says his only wish is that we keep moving in the same direction and I can't help it but right there in the back of my mind, despite my love, the achy love I have for him that rises, tugs me into his gravitational field, despite all that I see something sick and wounded I need to outrun.

TAKING TURNS

FRANKIE MCMILLAN

Because the Ferris wheel wouldn't start until all the seats were full we called out to Doreen to come join us and she looked up from her candyfloss and came running all doggish and eager until we told her she had to sit in her own seat, because she could be radioactive and even though it was long ago her father got an X-ray machine for his shoe shop; a black box you put your foot in and could see where the bone of your big toe met the tip of the shoe and your heel the back, the stories kept going round and round and each time we heard someone from our town had gotten cancer it was because they must have been to Clarke's shoe shop, even just walking past, the invisible rays could go right through you and when the Ferris wheel music finally started, the cogs and gears cranking and us swaying up to the very top, Doreen was always below, her eyes shut tight and then as we circled down we flung back our heads urging the Ferris wheel upward again.

"Laugh, Doreen," we cried, "laugh."

And then for a brief time Doreen was up and we

were down and she had a long-haired boyfriend who operated the go-karts and she'd look at us as if she knew something we didn't and once her boyfriend came up behind her and put his long tattooed arms around her waist and Doreen laid her glowing face against his shoulder, but all the time looking at us in a funny sort of way. "You don't know what you're missing," she said and we felt the sort of emptiness where the big ride fills fast and we're left behind the fence with tired legs, clutching out tickets that shred to pieces in our hot sticky palms before our turn eventually comes round again.

Frankie McMillan is a poet and short fiction writer from Aotearoa New Zealand. Her most recent book, *The Father of Octopus Wrestling and other small fictions*, was listed in Spinoff as one of the ten best New Zealand fiction books of 2019. Recent work appears in *Best Microfiction 2021* (Pelekinesis), *Best Small Fictions 2021* (Sonder Press), *Poetry New Zealand Yearbook* (Massey University), *New World Writing*, *Cleaver*, *Flash Boulevard* and *Atticus Review*.

BITTER HOT CHOCOLATE

SUDHA BALAGOPAL

The doctor laughs when my ten-year-old says her throat is too narrow to swallow the chunky pill for her ear infection, but I convince him her gullet tightens around the tablet until she cannot breathe, so he asks her to open wide, shines a flashlight, then says there's nothing physically wrong, plenty of room for the antibiotic to slide down, but, once home, she makes gagging sounds, wraps fingers around her neck, and turns beet red when she must take her medicine, so I'm forced to call the physician, who chuckles and says I should stir the pill into hot chocolate, at which I gasp, and he says he's not joking, so I buy the fanciest Swiss package, dissolve the medicine into the beverage, and my daughter swallows the frothiness, licks the mustache off her upper lip, and remarks that the creamy chocolate is bitter, but tasty, to which I respond, that's chocolate for you, and because she grins, after the course of antibiotics ends, I add to her Minnie Mouse mug multivitamins, cough medicine, even anti-diarrheals on occasion, so she believes this is good chocolate, the drink everyone loves despite the taste, and I tell her it's sort of how beer is popular, how people love it, and I shouldn't have used that particular comparison, because too soon, at sixteen, she begins to relish beer, and before I absorb the beer situation she gets attached to this guy who has a pungent temper and a delicious smile, a wild man who cannot be tamed, a creature all her friends adore, and she swallows his temper, his hot words, his beatings, his cheatings, but won't let go of him, even when I say she should, even after I introduce her to an upright young man, who on their first date places a cup of unadulterated hot chocolate before her, but she accuses him of doctoring the beverage, screaming that it tastes all wrong before she goes back to find that fellow with the pungent temper, so I call the doctor and tell him he should never again recommend mixing medicine into a beverage, and he responds, no laugh, there are reflexive actions involved in swallowing; fixing those is beyond his medical expertise.

Sudha Balagopal's short fiction has been published, or is forthcoming, in *CRAFT*, *Flash Fiction Online*, and *SmokeLong Quarterly* among other journals. She is the author of a novella-in-flash, a novel, and two short story collections. More at www.sudhabalagopal.com.

YOUR LIFE AS A BOTTLE

SARAH FRELIGH

Closing time, you hang out with the dishwashers who keep a bottle tucked behind the toilet tank in the employee's restroom, something rotgut and lowdown that tastes of Lysol and piss. A shot or two does the trick, makes it so you don't hate the cute girls with good teeth and cleavage delivering last-call martinis to rich guys while you're stuck in the kitchen refilling condiments. You're superstitious enough to pinch salt over your shoulder whenever you spill it, fool enough to whisper a wish. You marry your ketchups in a little ceremony—*Who takes this woman*—though it's less a commitment and more like pickup sex, random bottles tipped together lip to lip, each bleeding quick and urgent into the other while their caps stew clean in scalding water. Later you'll head to a bar where you'll drink yourself pretty under the black light of the dance floor. Later you'll find somebody to tip yourself into, an anybody who will empty you out and leave you clean.

RISE

SARAH FRELIGH

Weeks after the water rose, objects floated up from the drowned city below us: A baby shoe, a Starbucks mug, a red plaid dog collar tufted with wet fur.

Once there were eleven of us, once there were fish and berries. The water rose and rose. We used to see boats in the distance. Now we crowd together, ration what we eat. We dream of food hot from the oven, but wake to a cold smear of sun.

Books float up, beach themselves as if delivered: a manual on car repair and a mystery missing the last twenty pages. We spend a week arguing about the end. He did it; no, she did.

We vote when the moon is full. In summer, the moon is a ripe peach. Winter, a plate cold from the refrigerator.

We practice swimming every day, an hour in the morning and again before sunset. On clear days, we can see the buildings of the city below us, the spire of a church, the metal dome of what used to be the library.

Trucks used to deliver books. Their drivers parked in the middle of the street, flashers on, and carried boxes into the house. We stayed home for a year and the trucks brought us everything we needed.

The sun rises and falls. We quit counting long ago.

A strawberry moon, a red smear on the horizon that rises juicy, something to pull down and eat whole.

Kate today, Kate draws the short stick

The sun rises and falls. The water rises and rises.

Kate cries as she gives us what she took from before: A teething ring. A lock of hair. A silver thimble.

Once there was land. Once there was a beach where we spread towels and cooked food over fires and tossed Frisbies to dogs that nipped them from the air. The beach was sand and soft. We stood on the beach at the end of the day and applauded the sun setting over the water and then we drove home.

We hug Kate and say: *Swim hard. You're strong. Find help.* What we always say.

The dogs got old and died. We buried them with their Frisbies.

Home is a hill. There are three of us, the water is rising.

Sarah Freligh is the author of four books, including *Sad Math*, winner of the 2014 Moon City Press Poetry Prize and the 2015 Whirling Prize from the University of Indianapolis. Among her awards are fellowships from the National Endowment for the Arts and the Saltonstall Foundation.

CHICKEN-GIRLS AND CHICKEN-LADIES AND ALL THE POSSIBILITIES OF PILLOWCASES

EXODUS OKTAVIA BROWNLOW

In the earliest parts of the day, the chicken–girl saw all the possibilities of the pillowcases. Arms behind her, tucked into the slotted openness of the cases where the pillowcase held her arms as one, where they stretch without stinging because youth makes putty out of muscles.

When she runs around with her arms like that, the adults say—*Look, there she goes! There goes the little chicken–girl! Let's look at her fly. Let's listen to that bark.*

At this, the girl sticks out her bottom, wiggles and waggles it playfully. She ruffles her head where shaggy, feathered -bangs shake. When she jumps off stairs and stoops, she lifts a bit more each time.

It's good to be a chicken–girl, she screams.

It's wonderful that this is all I'll ever have to be.

In the latest parts of the day, the chicken–lady leaves the possibilities of the pillowcases behind her head. Arms by her sides, tucked into the slotted openness of a blanket where they fold as one over her stomach. When she stretches her body, there is a kind of stinging because ageing makes concrete out of muscles.

When she mopes around with her arms like that, the adultier-adults go—*Look, there she goes. There goes the chicken–lady. How often must we not see her fly? We have heard her once-beautiful bark, and now it is a crackly-rasped-wind, and no longer a bright-cheery-chirp.*

At this, the lady sticks out her bottom, smacks it hard where it splits the soft sounds of the room in half like an eggshell, and she separates herself away from them. She bonnets her head where frayed -bangs slither and knot underneath. When she jumps back into bed, she thinks about jumping off stairs and stoops again. She thinks about jumping from places where the ground cannot be seen so easily, and if that would be enough to see how much lift she has left.

It's wonderful to be a chicken–lady, she mumbles.

They told me to make angel wings out of these 'cases. Told me to inch my way toward being an eagle. But I think I'll stay here. I think this is all I'll ever want to be.

Exodus Oktavia Brownlow is a Blackhawk, Ms native. BA in English from MVSU. MFA in Creative Writing from MUW. Writer. Fashionista. Seamstress. Budding Beekeeper. You can find her work with *TriQuarterly, Electric Literature, Chicken Soup for The Soul, Booth, F(r)iction*, and more. She adores the color green, and a well-crafted gown.

IN THE TOWN WHERE ALL THE FINAL GIRLS LIVE

MEGHAN PHILLIPS

It is always fall, a permanent October. The leaves are always golden and crisp and falling falling falling. There are piles of leaves on lawns, still green and plush despite the chill in the air. There are friendly men with rakes and flannel shirts that wave when you walk by. There are other men standing behind bushes and crouched next to car fenders and lurking lurking lurking under windowsills at dusk.

In the town where all the final girls live, there are pumpkins on porches, all kitchen-knife carved. The soft glow of the tea lights spilling from their mouths. There are white picket fences, posts like the most perfectly straightened teeth. Gates that latch but don't lock. Gates that rattle when a car goes by just a little too fast or when a breeze blows just a little too hard or when an unfamiliar hand fumbles with the catch.

In the town where all the final girls live, something bad is happening. Something bad has already happened.

In the town where all the final girls live, there are second floor windows with curtains drawn back. Cracked open just a bit so the cool air can come in and the warm lamplight can trickle out. There are girls in their rooms deciding what to wear to meet their boyfriends, to party in the woods, to babysit down the block at the Johnsons'. There's a feeling they are being watched. That there is something just beyond the lemon pool of light on the grass. Something waiting waiting waiting for them to come out.

Meghan Phillips is the author of the chapbook *Abstinence Only* (Barrelhouse) and her stories have appeared in *Barrelhouse*, *Hobart*, and *Wigleaf* among other places. She was a 2020 National Endowment for the Arts literature fellow. Meghan lives in Manheim, PA with her husband and kids.

WRITER'S JEOPARDY

PAUL BECKMAN

Alex, out of the hospital with his cancer diagnosis, was standing holding the IV pole with one hand and maybe questions and answers in the other. I was one of three writers and back for my second day as returning champion. My mother was sitting in a chair off to the side with a spotlight on her. She had died of cancer a number of years earlier.

Alex began by introducing my mother and asking her what brought her to the show and she reached down and patted a large bamboo basket with a sign reading, *gift basket*. He asked her how she thought I did on the earlier show. She unwrapped a stick of Blackjack gum, popped it in her mouth and shrugged her answer back to Alex. Alex read off the headings and me, being the reigning champion, I got to go first,

"Alex, I'll take threats for $300."

"What is, I'll break every bone in your body?"

Barb buzzed first. "What did Paul's mother frequently say to him to show extreme displeasure?"

This was the right answer and my mother glared

at me as the audience applauded.

"Alex, I'll take threats for $400."

Tomasz buzzed in. "What is, for lying I'll wash your mouth out with kosher soap?" Again, the right answer and they were coming from the other writers and not me.

"Alex, sarcasm for $600 please."

"If _________ mother lets him jump off the bridge does that mean I have to let you jump too?"

Tomasz, lightning fast on the buzzer said, "Who is Myron?"

"Right again."

Tomasz, "Alex, I'll take guilting for $1000."

"Daily Double, Tomasz."

"Let's make it a true Daily Double, Alex."

"Tomasz, this could do it for you. Folks he's all in for $22,000."

"What is—I wish I were dead."

My mother looked at me with a self-satisfied look as the audience applauded.

Then the nurses came and escorted Alex out of the studio as the other writers went over and talked to my mother who laughed along with them. My Aunt Libby drove onto the stage in her Volkswagen

Beetle and my mother materialized in her sister's passenger seat and they drove off with my mother lighting up and blowing smoke rings to the applause of the audience.

Paul Beckman's latest flash collection, *Kiss Kiss* (Truth Serum Press) was a finalist for the 2019 Indie Book Awards. He had a story selected for the 2020 National Flash Fiction Day Anthology line up. He was nominated for 2021 Best of the Net and Best Microfiction.

BEFORE SHE WAS MY MOTHER

BOB THURBER

At eighteen, after winning two local beauty pageants, she hitchhiked to Hollywood, auditioned for a movie role with just one line, landed the part, but production fell through. Then she became pregnant. On all my birthdays she whispered that one line, smiling while adjusting her pose, searching for the spotlight.

Bob Thurber is the author of six books, including *Paperboy: A Dysfunctional Novel*. His work has appeared in *Esquire* and other magazines, been anthologized 70 times, received a long list of awards, and been utilized in schools and colleges throughout the world. He resides in Massachusetts. Visit http://www.bobthurber.net.

FOR A WIDOW

FRANCES GAPPER

It's ok to be angry. Ok to sit close to the track of a high-speed railway line, wings folded and legs tucked under. Ok to delay twenty-three trains for fifty minutes the day before Christmas Eve. Ok to ignore their attempts at persuasion/negotiation. Ok not to give a fuck.

As firefighters work to detach your Love's remains from the overhead line it's ok to feel numb, or not feel anything. Whatever humans think is correct swan behaviour ("mourning her mate") you're the expert re. you. When they advance holding a safety blanket it's ok to go for them.

You're a survivor. Just do that for a while, survive.

It's nice on the river.

Another swan, likewise bereaved (men smashed eggs and wrecked nest, she died of a broken heart), keeps appearing. Forget it, buster.

Ok not to show grace of movement, ok to be muddied and yank up weeds.

Ok to admire his persistence, ok to like him, fine

to accept from his beak tokens of esteem, tidbits he's saved for you. Ok to think you could love again, it's possible.

Ok to decide but no. Ok in late autumn when mist lies on the river to fly away.

Frances Gapper lives in the UK's Black Country. Her micros "Plum Jam" and "She's Gone" appeared in *Best Microfiction 2019* and *2021*. Her story "Lawn" placed second in the University of Kent Fiction Prize 2021 and she has been published fairly recently in *Blink Ink*, *Twin Pies Literary*, *Truffle* and *Sledgehammer Lit.*

THE HISTORIAN

ANDREW BERTAINA

The past cannot be rewritten, his wife said ominously as she stirred the dry oats into a morning bake. He was a historian though and knew this to be untrue. As such, after breakfast, he retired to his room and looked out into the garden, admiring the peonies and the overgrown bay bush, and then began writing his autobiography. In this version of his life, he got married to a woman vastly different than his longtime wife—this time he was married to a lovely French-speaking woman who supported his idleness, his predilection for explaining movie plots, his inability to put together IKEA furniture, and his fascination with silent cinema of the early twentieth century. And yet, as a house wren swooped across the yard, he suddenly found himself arguing with his seemingly pliant French wife about the name of one of his children. The two of them quarreled in his autobiography, and she sulked in her room. She was given to sulks, which vexed him greatly. And eventually they didn't have any children at all and separated. He couldn't remember why he'd married his French wife to begin with. She was very different than he'd expected. Sometimes he'd stay awake at night and dream of the coast of Maine, his old wife, who he'd written out of this version of history. He wondered if Herodotus had similar problems while composing *The Histories*. He suspected not. He just lacked a certain zest for life or so his French wife had always reminded him.

Andrew Bertaina's short story collection *One Person Away From You* (2021) won the Moon City Short Fiction Award. His work has appeared in *The Threepenny Review*, *Witness*, *The Normal School*, *No Contact*, and *The Best American Poetry*. He has an MFA from American University in Washington, DC.

LIGHTWEIGHT

BRETT BIEBEL

I was supposed to marry this girl whose brother won a Division III wrestling title, and she took me to see him once, at some big meetup near St. Cloud. He made weight at 133, and, honestly, he didn't look like much. Like a cornstalk, maybe. A ribbon of interstate late at night, and the reflective paint is hitting your face in strips, and he had the first kid he saw on the mat in about twelve seconds and then stared at the two of us up there in the bleachers like we were insects, crepuscular moths or something, and, later, between bouts, I was eating a hot dog, and Melissa was in the bathroom, and he came over to me and started talking about atoms, about how many there were in the human body and how they were all changing all the time and moving all across space, and he said somewhere inside him was this tiny piece of Hannibal Barca's dying breath, and he could channel it at will, he said, and everything felt static for a minute. Palms slapped foam. Bodies collided. Somebody was limping away from his match, and I could feel the bun collapsing in my hand, and now his face looked more like an exam, a word problem or a blue book, and I don't know what I said, but it wasn't anywhere close. It must have been as wrong as anyone can possibly be.

Brett Biebel teaches writing and literature at Augustana College in Rock Island, IL. His (mostly very) short fiction has appeared in *Hobart*, *SmokeLong Quarterly*, *Wigleaf*, and elsewhere. *48 Blitz*, his collection of flash fiction set in Nebraska, is available from Split/Lip Press.

A HAUNTING

BEN BLACK

The three of us haunt a house. We can do it because we're three. When we work together, they can hear us: we creak a floorboard, we slide a cup off its saucer, we disarrange the flowers in a vase. But it's not a proper haunting. They're not afraid. The old woman thinks we are a relative trying to send her a message. She lights candles to us and whispers questions in the night. She begs for our help. We can't haunt her—she loves us too much. The young woman ignores us: she brushes us aside as she goes through the house, she closes doors we open. Sometimes we annoy her, but mostly we don't faze her at all: she's too busy to be haunted. We spend most of our days between these two, not getting what we need from either. Only the maid, when she comes, seems uneasy: she shivers when she feels us near and every creak and rattle turns her head. She seems a perfect specimen. But we can't haunt properly when she's in the house: the old woman and the young woman are always there too. Three of them and three of us. Who knows what power they possess between them? Three of us with all our energy can move the dangling pans so they rattle in the night; what could three living beings do to us? We don't want to find out.

So when the maid is there we keep our distance, we tread lightly, afraid to catch her notice, afraid to unite those three against us, afraid they'll all turn toward us at the same time and catch us in the hot, wet prisons of their cavernous eyes.

Ben Black is an Assistant Fiction Editor at *AGNI*. He holds an MFA from SFSU and teaches English and writing in the Bay Area. His stories have appeared in *The Southampton Review*, *New American Writing*, *Wigleaf*, *Harpur Palate*, and *The Los Angeles Review*, among others. See more at benpblack.com.

SHY, SOLITARY ANIMALS

KRISTIN BONILLA

She drove down Cherry Hill Road, far enough away from the spot where some little girl's body was found naked, dumped by a man who stole her from her bedroom. There was a bend in the road she liked, a turnout with a wide expanse of valley below. The boy in the passenger seat ran his hand down her thigh.

She pulled her mother's '57 Corvette into the gravel. The gift a widow gives herself.

"Here?" he asked.

Earlier that day, a school assembly, rows of gawky teenagers seated on the gym floor. They walked a mountain lion onto the stage, chained, a wide metal collar around her neck. They said you had to be aware at all times when out in the hills. Mountain lions are silent killers, they said.

"Why don't they have an assembly about men stealing girls from their bedrooms," the girl next to her had whispered.

Female mountain lions are called queens, they said.

The queen yawned.

In the car, "Morning Dew" on the radio.

She straddled his lap.

"Did you know," she said, "the Grateful Dead didn't write this song? It was written by a woman. Bonnie Dobson. Everyone thinks it's about lovers parting the morning after, but it's not."

She put her hand across his throat, dragged her fingertip from the hollow of his neck to his belt.

"What's it about?"

"The morning after nuclear disaster. Sounds of the dying. Being the only man and woman left on the earth."

Their parents thought they were studying.

The scent of eucalyptus trees in fire season. Movement in the gravel behind the car.

They said if you see a mountain lion, it's already too late.

Kristin Bonilla's work has been nominated for Best Small Fictions, Best of the Net, and the *Wigleaf* Top 50 Longlist. She is an associate flash fiction editor at *jmww*, lives in Houston, TX, and is currently working on a novel. Follow her @kbonilla and read more at www.kristinbonilla.com

WOBBLE

PETER ANDERSON

The earth's had one too many and can't find her way home. Taxis aren't stopping. She broke a heel in the club and keeps slipping off the parking meter she's leaning against. She's got our names all wrong and keeps insisting I'm an Aries. I tell her not according to that constellation. *What?* Look up there that's Taurus. Aries has already been and gone. *Fucking god of war,* she mumbles, *wait a minute what time is it?* It's late. She stops searching for her phone and looks at us like who are we? We keep standing there, me and my friends, waiting for her to crash to the sidewalk scattering change from her purse and ice from her drink but somehow she never does. Somehow she always manages to right herself at the last minute. And each time she does, she laughs and says *that was close.*

Peter Anderson is a poet, performer and playwright who was born and raised in the suburbs of Detroit, attended the University of Michigan and now lives in Vancouver. His work has appeared in *Unbroken, Sublunary Review, The American Journal of Poetry* and others.

CORDS

ISABELLE B.L

I'm a whale, a bell and a multifunctional cord.

Today, I receive something to make my waist smaller. The giver says:

"It's made with 98 whale bones, my dear."

Hands of a woman I can't see thread black cords, in and out, pulls and ties. My feet enter a circle of jade and white lace. I'm a church bell. Ding-dong. He wants to see me.

My right arm slides down the mahogany rail. With each step, he adds an adjective. Breath-taking. Beautiful. Bewitching but I can only feel breathless.

The painter sees many church bells. Blue bells, golden bells, white bells or jade bells bordered with white lace.

I lay before him. I'm cordless. I'm free but only for an hour a day. He threads slowly, pulls gently and ties reluctantly.

They tell me not to read. They tell me not to write. They tell me not to paint. They tell me not to go outside, but like Eve, I'm curious.

Unfinished painting. My cordless body will never complete his canvas.

I pace back and forth. I speak to objects because they understand. I pretend my dinner plate is a ball. Shattered bodies. Shattered porcelain. Same thing.

Screams from cheek*less* faces, twig-like arms, bodies that slither. We become the names they call us.

A writer visits us today. We tell him our crimes. Nos with exclamation marks, an opinion too many, a wish for a cordless body. We want to breathe like a man. Can he write all that?

Waiting is hoping. I wait under the table with my head buried between my arms. Who will read our stories? Will anyone come for us?

I stand on the table and see naked trees.

I stand on the table and see April showers.

I stand on the table and see trees in full bloom.

I stand on the table and see a red, yellow and orange impressionist landscape.

One day, I can no longer straighten my legs, reach the iron bars and see—colour. I lay in the dark. I'm finally cordless but I'm not free.

Isabelle B.L has published a novel inspired by the life of a New Caledonian feminist. Her work can be found in the *Birth Lifespan Vol. 1* and *Growing Up Lifespan Vol. 2* anthologies for Pure Slush Books, *Flash Fiction Magazine*, *Visual Verse* and elsewhere.

SWAMP THING EXPLAINS HOW TIME PASSES IN THE MIDDLE OF DUELING CRISES

JACK B. BEDELL

It's never a matter of value. When I'm standing at the edge of the cypress grove looking over the coastline, I can tell it's receding, inching back into the swamp. No doubt the water's rising. It'll drown us all. Eventually. It'll lick away every piece of swamp I stand on. But it'll do it with the leisure of a glacier. There's time, always. And then from the boat launch a woman screams like her life depends on it, and choice disappears. You go instantly. No thought. No time for theory or data or analysis. On the dock, a scientist has gone mad having drunk his own formula. He's chased the dress half off this screaming woman. And she needs your help, now. Time evaporates into the sky, and this moment of crisis demands you act. It's not that the woman's life is somehow paramount, her loss more important than the coast's. It's just that her screams boil all time away, and a scientist is always easier to break than bad habits.

Jack B. Bedell is Professor of English and Coordinator of Creative Writing at Southeastern Louisiana University where he also edits *Louisiana Literature* and directs the Louisiana Literature Press. His latest collection is *Color All Maps New* (Mercer University Press, 2021). He served as Louisiana Poet Laureate 2017-2019.

GIVER OF GIFTS

JEFF FRIEDMAN

Before the old man went under, he sang one of his miserable songs, for which he is famous. He praised onions for their character, ducks for their communal spirit, and carpenter ants for their strong jaws and endurance. "So what if they don't win any races." He kissed each of us on the cheek, "for the last time," he said, his breath stinking of horseradish and garlic. "Be kind," he said, which he never was. He praised chicken fat, the four bellies of the cow, the croaking frogs that "scared the shit out of Pharaoh," with whom he split lox and bagel at the Carnegie deli on Wednesdays. He cursed the evil demented president and all his sycophants. He cursed the confederate senator blocking every bill, his wattle trembling, the attorney general bloating like a stuffed turkey. He begged us to follow the righteous path and give up vanity. He asked that we light candles for him, repeat his words, tell stories of his life. He asked that his memories become seeds that we plant in the wind. He called himself the last Babylonian king, spreading literacy to the masses. He called himself a "giver of gifts," though he never donated to any causes or even dropped a nickel in a beggar's cup. He praised himself for his journey in the desert, his days running with the hyenas, his devotion to a small bird that died in his hand. Then he closed his eyes and went under. At last, there was no pulse or breath, no preaching, only peace. But in the morning, he began to sing another of his miserable songs, and before he went under again, we had to repeat the whole damn ceremony.

Jeff Friedman has published eight collections of poetry and prose, including *The Marksman* and *Floating Tales*. He has received an NEA Literature Translation Fellowship and numerous other awards. Meg Pokrass and Friedman's co-written collection of micros, *House of Grana Padano*, will be published by Pelekinesis in April 2022.

CHICKEN DINNER

MORGAN BENNETT

In the night, our stepfather has us line up on the patio. Barefoot on the cold concrete, we are here to see him kill a chicken. This will mature us into adults. It's good for us to know about death, he told our mother, and so she does not stop him.

He wrings the chicken's neck to teach us how we will one day twist the necks of our enemies, or our children. Then he cleaves the head from the body. He looks at us meaningfully, although—meaning what?

I am standing on a rock almost small enough to be inconspicuous. I'm afraid to shift, so I continue to smother the pebble with my big toe, and it bites me back in self-defense. Now our stepfather has begun roughly plucking the bird, tearing out handfuls of feathers at random, action uninhibited by strategy. He throws them everywhere. Blood droplets fly with them and land on the white outdoor furniture. Two drops land by my sister's foot. A feather sticks in my brother's hair.

We will not eat the chicken. Later we will go inside, and our stepfather will light the corpse on fire in a child-grave-sized hole he dug in the backyard. We, the children, will go to bed. We will sleep and wake up and eat something that is not the bird, and so on, and so forth, and on and on, etc.

Morgan Bennett is an Austin, Texas-based writer and filmmaker. They spend too much money on coffee, and when they aren't writing, they enjoy watching movies and collecting skeleton decor.

ALICE, SOME OF THE TIME

ABBIE BARKER

Sometimes Alice waits at the end of her driveway for the bus. Sometimes she stomps in the slush, water seeping through the cracks of her boots, and she spends the day in damp socks. Sometimes Alice takes too long picking through her hamper for something clean, or mostly clean, and she has to ride to school in her mom's Subaru. Sometimes the Subaru smells like skunk. Sometimes Alice's mom jokes that Alice was late to her own birth. Sometimes Alice's mom grinds her teeth without saying anything, searching the rear-view mirrors, the side mirrors, for cars that aren't there. Sometimes her mom drifts over the rumble strip while tapping her phone, and Alice imagines swishing into a snowbank. Sometimes Alice imagines the car slamming into an oncoming truck, the airbags inflating with a hiss, bits of windshield skidding across the dash. Sometimes Alice wonders how it would feel to wake up in a hospital. Instead, she wakes up alone in her twin bed, missing her dad's warm palms.

Alice's dad never calls.

Sometimes Alice waits at the top of her driveway for a senior named Tyler to pick her up in his Jeep. Sometimes Tyler brushes the side of her leg when he shifts gears, his knuckles tepid and damp on her skin. Sometimes Alice presses her face on the passenger-side window so she can feel the chill against her cheek. Sometimes Tyler swerves while he sips his Starbucks and Alice wishes she could slap the cup away, spilling hot liquid across Tyler's crotch. Sometimes she imagines his Jeep plummeting to the bottom of an icy river, a tower of bubbles floating to the surface. Sometimes Alice drives herself to school in her mom's Subaru, reeking of smoke, and before she slides the car into reverse, she checks every mirror again and again. Sometimes Alice's mom asks if Alice is okay. Sometimes Alice digs through her mom's medicine cabinet, twisting the lid off every prescription, and later she forgets to twist the lids back on. Sometimes Alice wakes up in hospitals. Sometimes the blank walls and scratchy blankets make Alice miss her dad's fickle warmth, how seeing him every other holiday was almost enough. Sometimes Alice's mom squeezes her daughter's wrists and says, *I wanted so much more for you.* Her hands are always cold.

Abbie Barker is a creative writing instructor living with her husband and two kids in New Hampshire. Her flash fiction has appeared in *The Cincinnati Review*, *Hobart*, *Monkeybicycle*, *Pithead Chapel*, *The Citron Review*, and others. Read more at abbiebarker.com.

THE FLOOD

MATT BARRETT

The night my Pop-Pop's apartment flooded, he said, "I don't really believe I'm here," which I assumed meant here, in my bedroom, lying on a bare mattress, with a single pillow I'd found for him in my closet. "You'll go home tomorrow, Pop-Pop," I said. But this was not the kind of here he meant. The day he died, he told my mother, "I don't know why we keep doing this," and my mother smiled the way she smiled when she did not understand.

"What's *this*, Dad?" And he said, "This thing where we pretend I'm still alive."

When I found him in his apartment, his papers floated in the water. A Birth Certificate and cash, love letters from my grandma. He sat on the couch, the water rising past his waist. When I called to him from his window, he did not bother to look at me. I climbed inside, swam between his things. The doctors all said he was fine, he could spend the night with me.

"But don't you want to keep him?" I asked.

And they smiled, the way my mother smiled, when

she did not understand.

"He's yours," they said. "Why should we have to keep him?"

When my first child, my only child, was old enough to ask questions, I told him about that night. He asked me to tell the boat story again. I'd mentioned how Pop-Pop's walls were covered in wood, how his room took on the ocean as it rose. I guess he pictured it as a boat. The waves crashing, all his treasure lost.

The sound the ocean makes—when it blankets the stones and recedes. The constant swelling, the endless retreat. My son, he takes the foam that washes up and wears it like a beard. I tell him he looks good, even as an old man. He hunches his back, pretends to walk slowly. He plays this game for hours. And when it's dark and he's tired, we lay our backs against the stones and I dream each one is kissing me, kneading me, every pebble and grain of sand, asking if we'll stay.

Matt Barrett lives in Pennsylvania with his wife and two sons and teaches creative writing at his undergraduate alma mater, Gettysburg College. He holds an MFA in Fiction from UNC Greensboro and is currently at work on a YA novel.

GOING DOWN

TIM CRAIG

The elevator is between the twenty-first and the twenty-second floor when the cable snaps, so the passengers have some time to share their life stories before they hit the ground.

"I married too young," says the woman with the red hair and the butter-soft gaze and the lapel badge which reads "Baby on Board".

"I am likeable, and I am loveable," the middle-aged man in the cream shirt and brown tie says over and over, like a mantra. The red-haired woman notices he has missed a bit of his chin with the razor.

"If I had stayed in Inverkeithing," says the skinny guy with the safety pin through his eyebrow, "perhaps people would have bought my photographs."

"When I was a child of about eight," says the elderly woman in the blue coat, "there was a violent lightning storm one night while I slept. My mother woke me up to take out all the metal curlers from my hair."

"I *am* eight," says a little girl holding a grubby pink wallaby, "but I'm going to be nine in December."

There are two other passengers in the elevator, but they do not have enough time to tell their stories; inevitably in such situations, someone always ends up disappointed.

Tim Craig lives in London. A winner of the Bridport Prize for Flash Fiction, his short-short stories have been placed or commended four times in the Bath Flash Fiction Award, and have appeared in literary magazines in both the UK and the US, as well as *Best Microfiction 2019.*

CHICKENS IN THE PARLOR

ROBERT SCOTELLARO

Moat In Lieu of a Welcome Mat

When my mother felt her life had become drab and spark-smothered, her lipsticks became redder and redder.

And she built a moat around the house. Each day when my father came home from scrubbing graffiti off subway station walls, he'd swim through a clinging storm of mosquitoes to get to the front door with one hand paddling, the other holding his bottle of whiskey above the brine.

Old MacDonald

Mother sprinkled feed on the rug for the chickens in the "parlor." (What she called that tiny room with a convertible sofa in it.) The chickens hopped up onto the furniture knocking things over. I was young and didn't mind their ceaseless pecking. My father found a burial plot inside the newspaper and started digging, so he never noticed the new dress Mother was wearing or the candy apple red high heels. "This is what you get when you act like Old MacDonald," Mother said, sweeping her arm broadly and causing a few chickens to flutter feckless wings. "Ee-i-ee-i-o," she said.

Steam Scream

Mother rid the house of chickens, and Dad learned to cha-cha-cha. (It's strange to think how old they seemed then—how young they really were.) They were in the kitchen dancing when the teapot started screaming. Father turned, but Mother said, "Leave it." That she didn't want to stop for a single minute, that those red high heels were out of their coma. She was wearing a flared sundress and Father had on his grey razor-creased trousers with high cuffs. I found a quarter once in one of those cuffs as they draped over a chair. It was an archeological high point.

Father seemed to like the way that dress bell-shaped as she twirled, and the feel of it—the tea kettle, not so much. A record skipped on the turntable, was stuck in a brassy repetitious snippet over and over... Father turned again, sweating at that point.

"Leave it," Mother said.

Robert Scotellaro's work has been widely published in print and online journals and anthologies. He's the author of seven chapbooks and five flash fiction collections. Two new collections are forthcoming in 2022. He has, with James Thomas, co-edited *New Micro: Exceptionally Short Fiction* (W.W. Norton, 2018). Visit him at: www.robertscotellaro.com.

HISTORY LESSON

JENZO DUQUE

the thing about catholic school is no one wants to talk about how Columbus left in chains frankly it's embarrassing but already we get the monday off and who doesn't like a four day week i mean look see the meek will inherit the earth and that's why things went so well for indians they each got a cut of the pumpkin pie and cornucopia can you say it with me cornucopia c-o-r-n-u-c-o-p-i-a cornucopia can you use it in a sentence yes cesar please dazzle us ok this class is a cornucopia of bull shit

bull shit is not one of the things you can say haven't we taught you better by now this is how you carry yourself this is how you dress to avoid confrontation this is how you address authority so as to avoid confrontation this is how you color nice and neat in between the lines this is how you sign your signature this is how you send a letter this is how you take a quiz this is how you take a test this is how you take a punishment this is how you take god's grace this is how you ask god to save your soul this is how you burn energy this is how you run outside in circles until the world blurs around you and you can hear him right the singing and those textures in the air

it's in the air across all frequencies indistinct chatter takes to the streets and what is it about rising temperatures and that lake effect flicker that makes them so restless dark skin flaring up in alleyways or under overpasses think of the westside riots and the beat of the national guard's drum the hum of the El above us elevated track racket kraa kraa pops on the rooftops someone's taking shots tune in tonight at 6:30 catch it live and by the toe and if he hollers if he hollers if he hollers well let im go

---

Jenzo DuQue is from Chicago and based in Brooklyn. His work has found homes in *Narrative*, *BOMB*, *Gulf Coast*, and elsewhere. Twice nominated for the Pushcart Prize, Jenzo's writing has been anthologized in *The Best American Short Stories 2021*. Read more at jenzoduque.com.

THE DRAGON AND IT

KATE FRANCIA

I was still rattly in my new skin when I ate the first one. He came through the gap in the rocks and saw *it* lying there, and gave this cry like I had bitten his heart in two, so I did.

I was treating it well, at the time. Its golden hair all spread out on a pillow. But I kept happening upon them pressing their lips against it, and honestly, that seemed rude. So I strung it up in a cage twenty feet off the ground. Didn't work. I was having to eat more of them than ever. Each time I ate one, my skin stretched.

Until one day, she came. Thin and grey, no armor, no challenge. She didn't run or scream. She saw it in the cage with its golden hair hanging down, and started crying. Unappetizing.

Then she looked at me. "Please," she said.

"Please what?" I said. I thought she was going to say "don't eat me."

"I know it's you, Gwen. Please come home."

I ate her immediately.

My stomach bulged. All wrong. My skin stretched so tight, something aching to get out, just like Before. All my memories bubbling up, piecemeal, with bites taken out of them.

I'd been holding onto *it*, all this time, thinking I might go back. I couldn't bear it. Her face, my name. I couldn't remember, and be *this*.

I pulled down the cage and looked at it.

Just a body, really. Bones and crunch.

Kate Francia's short stories have appeared in *Electric Literature*, *Beneath Ceaseless Skies*, *Lady Churchill's Rosebud Wristlet*, and elsewhere. You can find her at katefrancia.com.

IRON HANS

JULIE CADMAN-KIM

"Why is that man screaming?" my son asks, stopping midstride. He is almost five, and prone to anxiety.

"He doesn't know the difference between real and pretend," I tell him. The man is facing the plate-glass window of the new Whole Foods across the street. He's doubled over nearly in two, crying like he learned his mother was murdered. Crying like he learned he'd murdered his own mother. "Why'd you leave me alone?" he screams. His shoulders are covered in a sodden gray blanket, his feet bare even though it's February. "I told you I would do it. *I told you.*"

"Is he talking to us?" my son asks.

The sky, gray as the man's blanket, has been heavy and low for what seems like years.

"No," I say.

An attractive young couple walks past the man, stepping into the street to avoid him.

"Let me out!" the man pleads to his reflection. "Why did you leave me alone in here?"

My son's words are careful. "I think I know him."

"You've seen that man before?" I ask.

My son nods. "In our house," he says.

"That man has never been in our house," I say, but my mouth has gone dry and my palms are wet. There is something familiar about the hunch of the man's shoulders.

"He has too," my son says. He steps behind me and peers around my legs at the man.

"That's not true," I say, too sharply.

"It *is* true. He comes when you're asleep. He opens the window and climbs into my room."

Across the street, the man stops howling. He stands up straight, and the blanket falls from his shoulders. He looks at my son; something passes between them. The man holds up a hand covered in sores. He waves, then beckons.

My son's eyes are clear and bright. "His hands are made of metal," he breathes. "Look—they're rusty."

I look. And they are.

"He's crying because he wants his real hands back," my son says.

I imagine the man's hands are made of iron. He is a prince held captive by a spell, a curse. He was a little boy once, just like mine. Maybe, together, we can set him free.

I look down at my son. “We can’t give him his hands back,” I say. “We don’t know where they are.”

My son returns the man’s wave. “When he comes to my window tonight, I’ll give him mine. Then he won’t have to scream anymore.”

Julie Cadman-Kim is a writer from the Pacific Northwest. Her work has appeared or is forthcoming in *Catapult*, *McSweeney’s Internet Tendency*, *Black Warrior Review*, *Passages North*, and elsewhere. She currently lives in Ann Arbor while she pursues her MFA at the University of Michigan’s Helen Zell Writers’ Program.

EVERYTHING YOU EVER GAVE ME

MARY JONES

I picked up everything you ever gave me—those old books you bought from used bookstores for not very much money, and the shells you found on the beach when you were visiting California. I picked up the doubt you made me feel every day every time you seemed so involved with those other women and I'd ask you about it and you'd talk me out of believing what I knew to be true. I picked up the love I felt. I picked up always wondering where you were and what that spot on your neck was, and I picked up how small you'd make me feel sometimes, and for no good reason, and usually when I was feeling good about something else. I picked up your face and your body and your lies and your promises and I squeezed them together into a ball and threw it up into the sky over to the moon. And the people applauded.

Mary Jones's stories and essays have appeared in Electric Literature's *Recommended Reading*, *EPOCH*, *Alaska Quarterly Review*, *Columbia Journal*, *Gay Mag*, *Wigleaf*, *Southwest Review*, *Brevity*, and elsewhere. She holds an MFA from Bennington College and teaches fiction writing at UCLA Extension.

RUST BELT TRIPTYCH

LAUREN KARDOS

I. Effect

Pierogi mother heaves groceries in the supermarket checkout line when her dress seam catches on the cart's rusty corner. Starchy potato breasts, a belly of melted cheese, and lardy legs flash the tabloid and crossword puzzle towers. Even the Big Red gum blushes. The employee chews her lip, informs pierogi mother the check bounced. Normal husbands leave surprises of new clothes, functioning bank accounts, tidied kitchens. Her husband was a nimbus cloud, raining down red and minus signs across town. Provide. Solve. Care. How many jobs can her half-naked shoulders bear? Pierogi mother abandons the Hamburger Helper™ ingredients on the conveyor belt and darts toward McDonald's across the highway. Ten dollars in quarters jangle in her purse.

II. Cause

Crow father is too busy tucking shiny garbage into the attic eaves to worry over errands, budgets, and bills. Instead, he flits about, weaving tunnels out of unsought commodities. Whitening toothpaste from a network marketing company, compilation jazz albums from midnight infomercials, diamond tennis bracelets too fragile for pierogi mother to wear to work. His black eyes shimmer, pride or fallen insulation tearing him up: not every father can predict a family's wants and needs. The repossession notice taped to the door he tosses into the backyard's burn pile. Over the phone, a bank representative is pleased to activate his new credit card.

III. Solution

Mouse child wiggles toward the cracked window, searching for a breeze. Sun rays tickle her eyelashes, bake the car seat plastic. She hums an invented tune, pigtails bopping and light-up sneakers keeping time on the middle console. If she behaves, pierogi mother promises, she can rent *Ghostbusters* at Video City again. Crow father promises the next bonus, the next paycheck, the next letter to Santa will deliver the fabled Universal Studios vacation. Year-round, mouse child plates cookies for Slimer. Her favorite ghost is green, hungry, and misunderstood—like her. She'd trade all the unasked-for princess dolls to ride the Spooktacular, wave to Slimer in real life. Pierogi mother crosses the parking lot with a Happy Meal® in hand. Molten air singes mouse child's lungs. She smiles. Today, she won't make a peep, won't whine, won't cry. For Slimer, she'd be a good girl and start hiding the coins she finds under her dresser.

Lauren Kardos (she/her) writes from Washington, DC, but she's still breaking up with her hometown in Western Pennsylvania. Her work has been featured in *Emerge Literary Journal, The Lumiere Review, Rejection Letters*, and elsewhere. Follow her on Twitter: @lkardos.

HER KINGDOM COME

KRISTEN ZORY KING

There was a funny turn to Mother's mouth when she saw the ants each summer, a tightness to the lips so that they were colored only by a faint over-layer of the paling pink tint she put on in the mornings. It was a color both too young and too old for her, evoking the light, pollen-like powder puffs of a more glamorous era and the uncertainty of a teenager who's just agreed to a ride home from the school quarterback. There were traces of it everywhere: a rosy blur on the rim of her milky coffee cup, the butts of half-ashed cigarettes. She even kissed-closed the notes she'd send along in our lunch boxes, a reminder of her love and the reach of her surveillance. Every July she'd stand at the window and watch as the ants made a steady and solid trail over the sink and toward any crumb my brother or father or I had left lingering, her eyes narrowed, her fingers holding a single bleeding ice cube to the soft pulse on her neck. She was quick with immediate attacks—white domed traps in every corner, bottles of Windex which flattened their small bodies on impact and left a chemical taste to the air—but her favorite, the most unforgiving, was boiled water. Circling the perimeter of the house, she'd calmly watch for any small movement, cracks in the sidewalk, a glowing blush from the sun on the back of her neck. And then she'd return to the kitchen with a walk I'd describe as relaxed if I didn't know better, couldn't see her shoulder blades arched sharp through the back of her summer linen, and place a large pot of water to boil on the stove. Once it hissed, she'd return to the spot, handling the grenade from the kitchen with yellow gloved hands and pouring the scalding liquid directly onto the shivering mass. *Only way to kill the queen*, she'd say, giving no consideration to the small burns rising in the naked space between her dress and house shoes. Task complete, she'd return to the house, taking her place by the sun soaked window to watch over her kingdom, something gleeful, dangerous sitting patiently in the small corners of her lips.

Kristen Zory King is a writer and teaching artist based in Washington, DC. Recent work can be found in *Electric Literature*, *The Citron Review*, *Emerge Literary Journal*, *(mac)ro(mic)*, and *SWWIM* among others. Learn more or be in touch at www.KristenZoryKing.com.

CANVAS

SCOTT GARSON

At first, he thought that his being made to stand guard by an empty canvas was some kind of joke, on him, on his worthlessness. He could take it. He was being paid. Then he arrived at a different idea: what if the joke was on everyone else? What if his being made to stand guard was the move that was needed to sell it? Draw in fools. Get them rubbing their chins. Finally he came to a thought that was more like a feeling, since it wouldn't cohere. He stood guard by an empty canvas in an empty wing at the end of a day. He could be real—an actual man—or theoretical. Who would know? The guard stepped away from his place by the wall. Blinking, he tried to see into the light of the canvas, like it was a mirror.

Scott Garson is the author of *Is That You, John Wayne?*—a collection of stories. He lives in central Missouri.

JUMP

ANDREA LYNN KOOHI

One day my best friend and I decide we've had enough of Barbies. We're sick of brushing butt-length blonde hair and dressing long plastic limbs in mini-skirts. So one day we tie long strings around their torsos and fling them out the window of the store-top apartment where I live with my mom. We let them dangle above the sidewalk for a minute or two and then reel them back in to see how they look. These, we see immediately, are changed Barbies. We admire their spunk and disheveled hair, and we like how they look like they've been somewhere, like the kids in our class who leave on trips our moms can't afford and then magically return somehow taller than before.

Soon our Barbies start talking about pot and tattoos and running away. We cut fringes into their clothing and dye their hair with purple Kool-Aid. And not a day passes without a jump out the window—their "don't give a shit" leap into the unknown.

One day a woman on the sidewalk screams when a Barbie descends head first from the window and comes to a halt in front of her face. We giggle as she yells at us for being hooligans and I pull the Barbie up fast in case she tries to grab it. It's fun surprising people, making them look up to the sheet-covered windows in the homes above the stores they never knew were there. Making them see that *we* are there.

We wait until the lady is well out of sight and toss our Barbies out the window again. This time, though, my Barbie comes loose from the string. She lands face-up on the dirty pavement, her hair like dead snakes around her staring head. There's a second where my friend and I stare back at the stillness, something snagged in our throats, before one of us laughs and we breathe again.

Andrea Lynn Koohi is a writer from Toronto, Canada. Her fiction and creative non-fiction have appeared in *filling Station*, *Pithead Chapel*, *The Maine Review*, *Lost Balloon*, *Whale Road Review*, *trampset*, *New World Writing* and elsewhere.

IT WAS 1687 WHEN AN APPLE FELL IN NATURAL MOTION

TANYA CASTRO

The galaxy sits in my palm. Only until it becomes a fist like watching a shark open his mouth and your life hanging on to nothing. There's a story my father would tell my brother and I as children, there was once nothing until there was genesis. My father would list creation and I saw how it sat on his tongue, in the way that the stars sit against space. Everything sits on atmosphere. On the third day, when dry land was created, there was finally something to sit against light and sky. A reflection was born. The trees were created as well. A shadow was born. My father still tells me the story. Only now, I know how creation feels. It sits against me as I sit against it. The story ends on the seventh day, when creation *finished* like the way I watch a galaxy disappear when there's nothing to hold on to. It was named gravity. The way humans fall.

Tanya Castro is a writer from Oakland, California. She holds an MFA in Poetry from Saint Mary's College of California. Tanya's work was nominated for Best of the Net 2021. Her work has appeared or is forthcoming in *The Acentos Review, Anser Journal, FEED, Lost Balloon* and Mason Jar Press.

UNFADING

NATHALIE HANDAL

She told me to find her in the room midway between life and death. Her hair wrapped in a rope of clouds tied to the sky. Her neck bent by a man's hand, her tongue suspended, one eye hidden and an old man trying to get everything he could from her mind. The telephone ran in her entire body and wires tugged her in different directions the way exile does. The way the world falls and the sea begs when love is limping. The way numbers climb the wind like death tolls when oppressors are free. Men tried to write her for a century, and other eternities. Their head spun in place. Their rage so loud she stopped hearing it. Then an Andean Condor came and stared. The walls started sweating blood. The dead always come alive if they didn't die right. Suddenly they were all there: Sor Juana Inés de la Cruz, Manuelita Sáenz, Juana Azurduy de Padilla, La Pola, Paixão Pagu, Tania La Guerrillera, las hermanas Mirabal, las Madres de la Plaza de Mayo, las Abuelas de la Plaza de Mayo. They were speaking about the myths, loading their words and singing songs she hadn't discovered yet. They were drinking coffee, smoking air. They said: *No one will tell you where the water begins in your body nor where the blue gets bluer. It's a question of power. Explore the ruins. Draw the maps of deaths and damages and desires. Dive into her deep. Deep into her erotic. Discover the way back to her dream, your dream, and we will never disappear.* After that, when men tried to take her clothes off, her sexiness off, her luminance off. She stared at them. An amaranthine stare.

Nathalie Handal is the author of seven prize-winning collections, including *Life in A Country Album*, winner of the Palestine Book Award; and the flash collection *The Republics*, lauded as "one of the most inventive books by one of today's most diverse writers," and winner of the Virginia Faulkner Award.

LET'S

L MARI HARRIS

not live here anymore. share orange slices and salted peanuts on Route 66. keep Merle Haggard on repeat. not bring up last year. not wonder who she would have looked more like. not go down that road. say Grace. stop at that roadside stand. talk to the man sitting there. listen to his stories of passing poets and spring tills and unexplained lights flickering in the night sky. buy the big box of yellow and orange and red tomatoes. fill our mouths, the juice running down our arms to puddle in our palms. kiss after we eat the last one. snap photos of each other in front of the world's biggest metal dinosaur. send a postcard to the roadside stand man: we get it now, our initials in a flourish. rewrite our book of revelations in a gentle font. find an old barn filled with hay. hunker down until the rains pass. not turn our bodies away from each other like yesterday, last month, last year. lock eyes again. make a steeple of our fingertips. remember how we stumbled into each other when we were both looking the other way.

GIRL AS MUSIC BOX BALLERINA

L MARI HARRIS

This girl writes with glitter pens, draws little glitter hearts next to her name, adds XOXO. Doesn't pick at her food and ask to be excused. Sings along to the radio, drums her fingers on the dashboard, catches her mother's smile and blows her a kiss. Wears her sleeves pulled down to her fingertips, doesn't look in the mirror when she undresses at night. Says "I don't know what I was thinking" when her mother stares at her too long. Smiles at her teachers when tests are handed back, raises her hand when questions are asked. Draws little daggers in her notebook. Smiles smiles smiles. Thrashes at night, grinds her teeth, digs her nails into her stomach, her thighs, her upper arms, screams in her dreams. This girl dances when she's opened. Spins until the lid is closed and she's folded back into the beautiful dark.

L Mari Harris's most recent work has appeared in *Milk Candy Review*, *CRAFT*, *Okay Donkey*, among others. She lives in the Ozarks. Follow her @LMariHarris and read more of her work at www.lmariharris.wordpress.com.

CODES TO LIVE BY

JUDE HIGGINS

We're communicating in semaphore now. Out on the lake with our red and yellow flags in separate little row boats. It takes most of the morning to spell out everything.

I suggest we vary things with morse code, but you interpret my message as "varying things with Norse Odes". Why you think poems about the Norse gods will help, I don't know. Nevertheless, we may have summoned up Thor, because it thunders and we return home to avoid being struck by lightning.

After the storm goes, we stand at opposite sides of the garden and get out our flags again. You sign to me that folk isolated in faraway mountains learned to communicate by whistling urgent news across great distances. I sign back to remind you I can't whistle. I suck in air instead of blowing it out. Also I have no head for heights. If you want to live in the mountains, you can go it alone.

You drop everything and rush out in a huff. I tow our rowboats to a nearby hill and make a bonfire, but I only know the smoke signal for "Help". Then

I have to fend off a party of Boy Scouts who run up the hill to rescue me. They're disappointed when they discover there's nothing wrong.

The boy scouts eat their sandwiches when the sun comes out and one of them spots the steady wink of a mirror in the distance. "I love you," he translates, blushing through his pimples. He's not old enough to have uttered those words out loud before. The other boys giggle and say it must be the girl at school he fancies, messaging him. He turns bright red. I remember when I used to blush and giggle. So long ago.

I drive home. You've bought flowers. We talk.

Jude Higgins' chapbook *The Chemist's House* was published by V. Press in 2017. Her flash fiction is published widely in magazines and anthologies. She founded Bath Flash Fiction Award and directs Flash Fiction Festivals U.K. and Ad Hoc Fiction.

SAME OLD (NOTES TO SELF)

JANEAN CHERKUN

The fridge vocalises like a dog: *yip yip yip*, or *yop yop*. But I'm the kitchen bitch. Water dripping somewhere invisible and cold, the stop-and-start conduit of the self-defrost function. It's a boring lexicon lesson, it's onomatopoeia, it's whiteware gone beige.

It's a domestic scene of extremes, with its soft, sad, expiration-driven ingredients, juggled and dropped each day, each week. Self-destruction also happens, but never homemade lunchbox treats. I am the gunk in the disgusting sandwich, 'cos sure as shit I ain't the bread.

I speak Fridge. I drip, I drop, I blip, I stop. I breathe complaints and instructions into a mirror with a cranky emoji staring back, so all the words are backwards and the semantics bosh. Leave mess on bench. Use all hot water for your own warmth and comfort, don't refill kettle. Discard fruit: flesh, skin and all, under old lady's tree on walk to school.

The sandwich dried out from the misappropriation of plastic wrap. The hot water bottle sprang a leak and the child woke in a puddle of water and sheets as soggy as cereal in a bowl.

The Saint Bernard or the Rottweiler may open her throat now and spill the dangers of running over rocks in melting snow, the hazards of ingesting raw meat. She'll growl and whine that in this place, the hydatid heart, the bins are full and funky and must go out to the street on Wednesday.

Janean Cherkun is a stenographer from the city of Dunedin in New Zealand. A fantastic place, so she writes about it; also sometimes about Russia, where she has travelled with her husband. She would eventually like to indulge her mind's eye view of Antarctica and write about that as well.

THROWING STONES

MICHAEL TODD COHEN

The Bastard Boy and his brother threw speckled stones—brick-red, tooth-white rimmed with yellow, mucus-green slicked with algae—into the angry swell of the Atlantic. The brother did not think of himself as a brother to this anxious bastard who knew nothing of baseball—*What's a crow-hop?*—how to arc his arm in a perfect parabola to send the stones as far into the cobalt blue as they could go, to land with a satisfying *glug!* a belch from the deep *glug! glug! glug!* One after another, the brother who did not think of himself as a brother, made an arc like a rainbow or a bridge or the door to a church and listened, seconds after: *glug!* and nodded at the incoming tide in satisfaction like a signal to a catcher crouching on the ocean floor holding up a web of kelp and waiting.

Crack! This is the sound made from rock on rock, when the Bastard Boy threw, never reaching water, like the meeting of a bat to ball, *crack!* so that even though he knew nothing of the game, one was being played in the pitch his brother, who did not think of himself as a brother, threw and the *crack!* that followed. Then quiet. And in this quiet the Bastard Boy thought of all the times he'd been thrown silence from the brother, who did not think of himself as a brother, when all he wanted was the *crack!* of his own name.

Michael Todd Cohen's work appears in *Columbia Journal*, *X-R-A-Y Literary Magazine*, *Pithead Chapel*, *jmww* and *HAD*, among others. His writing has been nominated for a Pushcart Prize. He lives with his husband and two dogs, by a rusty lighthouse, in Connecticut. You can find him on twitter @mtoddcohen or michaeltoddcohen.com.

CALLING AT: PHARMACY, FLORIST, AND OFF-LICENCE ONLY

LUCY GOLDRING

Strange to go against the flow, to squeeze through bodies hell-bent on bagging seats aboard a train going nowhere. *Mad* to abandon scores of sweaty commuters for-fuck's-saking in stifling carriages. *Peculiar* to say, "I forgive you," without asking what "*technically* it wasn't adultery" means. *Bizarre* to move on in mindless circles, like these new-bloody-fangled trains. *Odd* that Viagra ads plastered along your route will snap you out of it. *Demented* to abandon your thirty-year career mid-shift, your engine running hot. *Ludicrous* to be clattering down Marchmont Street towards your unsuspecting spouse—pills, peonies, and vino swinging wildly at your side.

Lucy Goldring is a Northerner hiding in South West England. She's been shortlisted by National Flash Fiction Day (NFFD) and won *Lunate*'s monthly flash competition once. Lucy was nominated for Best Small Fictions 2020 by both NFFD and *100 Word Story*. When not climate angsting she binges on sitcoms. www.livingallover.com.

BOWERBIRD

GABRIELLE GRIFFIS

In my grandmother's house I found ferns, dried and preserved from her wedding bouquet. She saved zinnia seeds and planted them in a seasonal loop. A good person's house decays as if they were never there. We inhabit one home to another like shells. In the living room I found books about fungi. The pages were full of wine caps and destroying angels. She hung holy basil and fennel from rafters. She painted sunflowers and foxgloves on the walls. In the cabinet were envelopes full of seeds, a camera, binoculars, pens, and empty greeting cards. Her clothing was made of cotton and wool. On the mantle was a lamp, candle sticks, quartz, cormorant feathers. In the bedside table were dream journals. She wrote she was looking at a spiderweb in a windowsill, a woman in a bathtub. A man stood over her in the darkness, his face full of sorrow. She wandered wetlands and hills, had a basement drawer full of bones, and an orange bottle of alprazolam. Vinegar solvents, baking soda, lemon oil. Mason jars full of rose buds and lavender. I made spearmint tea in an iron tea kettle and fingered a naturalist's portrait of a cephalopod on the piano. The jar of colored pencils was old, the banjo was worn. Sparrows waited on the doorstep for birdseed my grandmother told me to spread. Moss crawled through cracks in brick. I watered her wilting plants, waiting for the funeral home to carry her away. The gas stove turned on, warming candyleaf and hibiscus. A discarded drawing of a deer, yellowed with age read: *panic panic panic*. I opened a book from a cedar shelf full of phases of the moon. Her last breath lingered in the bedroom. A storm glass predicted rain. Men wheeled her through doorways, a metallic whine, a click, a sheet. Fallen leaves, milkweed floss floated in the air. Her dog whimpered as the hearse disappeared from the driveway.

Gabrielle Griffis is a multimedia artist, writer, musician, and librarian. Her work can be read in *Wigleaf*, *Split Lip Magazine*, *matchbook*, *Monkeybicycle*, *Gone Lawn*, *X-R-A-Y Literary Magazine*, *Okay Donkey*, and elsewhere. Visit her website at gabriellegriffis.com and follow her online at @ggriffiss.

PORK FLUFF

TIFFANY HSIEH

In the fifth-floor apartment of a building with no elevator, he was old and alone now because his wife had died first. One of his children lived nearby and arranged to have bento delivered to his door four times a week. Three times a week they had him over. Used to be three times bento and four times over when there were two of them. He didn't mind the new arrangement. He'd rather not eat at someone else's table, especially his daughter-in-law's. He never did like her cooking and his wife berated him every time he asked for pork fluff to go with his rice. She said if someone was going to have them over and feed them, especially their daughter-in-law, he should just be thankful and eat what was on the table. Now that he was old and alone because his wife had died first, he ate boiled broccoli for breakfast, doctor's orders. With each floret he added pork fluff right out of the bag. Sometimes fish fluff. He figured he would eat a whole plate of boiled broccoli if it meant he didn't have to sit on the toilet for a long time and be sore. He figured that was important in case there were more years left than necessary.

Tiffany Hsieh was born in Taiwan and moved to Canada at the age of fourteen. Her work has appeared in *The Los Angeles Review, The Malahat Review, Poet Lore, Room, Salamander, The Shanghai Literary Review*, and others. She lives in southern Ontario.

A GIRL MAKES LEMONADE

RUTH JOFFRE

Her life is a series of powders. Lemonade mix. Graphite. Ash. Everything in their kitchen was previously freeze-dried, flash-fried, concentrated, reconstituted, or saturated with some form of powder or irregular solid manufactured in a lab. Convenient sustenance, the packaging says. A chance to experiment, she thinks. On consumers. On lab rats. And on herself. After school, while her parents hustle from their first dead-end jobs to their second, she stands at the kitchen counter, testing her limits. Lemonade concentrate with ground rosemary? Delicious. Powdered coffee and activated charcoal? Pointless. Charcoal adds no value. She would rather paint with it. Smear it on her cheeks like bone dust. Pretend she is a necromancer raising spirits from the dead. She already reads most of her books by candlelight, does her homework as close to the window as possible to catch the setting sun. Their apartment has no electricity, no hot water. These are luxuries only the top Company-Polity in the region can provide its workers. Everyone else must be glad for a roof, a sink, sometimes a wall or a door to separate the toilet from the bed. When the sun goes down, a company candle will have to suffice. Only then does the apartment look big. Distant corners with the potential for clandestine meetings. Oblong shadows with no faces. Smoke whispering secrets, which the company can't hear, not yet. Not until all the other company kids are ready. Until then, she'll sharpen her pencils into shavings. Mold melted candle wax into marionettes. Stage puppet shows of lemonade stands where one puppet says *How much?* and then another says *It's free. All lemons should be free.*

A GIRL WISHES ON A STAR

RUTH JOFFRE

And who can say whether that star, in its capriciousness, decides to answer? Who can say with certainty that a random star picked on a chilly autumn night cannot harness all the mysteries of the cosmos and hear from hundreds of light years away this wish the girl dares not utter aloud, a wish so small and secret she only allows herself to think it once while sitting next to a campfire at half past midnight, after most of the other scouts from her troop have gone to sleep and left her almost alone with Silvia (Sil), her crush, who likes wearing shorts even in winter and knits funny hats for herself in the shape of little forest creatures and has never once shaved her legs, because, she says, "It's natural insulation. Why would I get rid of it?" And why wouldn't that star, given a minute to consider the girl where she sits, hugging her knees, casting her longing glances into the heart of the fire so the wrong person won't catch them—why wouldn't that star say, *Fuck it! This is an easy one*, then grant the girl's wish, which is not to be popular or to have perfect skin or get into her first choice of college but for Sil to sit next to her, just to sit beside her for a few minutes as autumn leaves fall around her in the starlight? Is that so much to ask?

Ruth Joffre is the author of the story collection *Night Beast*. Her work has appeared or is forthcoming in *Kenyon Review*, *Lightspeed*, *Pleiades*, *The Florida Review Online*, *Flash Fiction Online*, *Wigleaf*, *Baffling Magazine*, and elsewhere. She lives in Seattle, where she serves as Prose Writer-in-Residence at Hugo House.

GIRLS WHO SAT AT THE BACK OF BUSES

M. L. KRISHNAN

Girls who sat at the back of buses had names like Harini, Rose or Sindhuja. They sat cross legged—their feet protruding from the rexine-flaked upholstery, humming with purpose. They mushed their bodies into spherical brinjals, thickets of children, ductile bands of ribbon fish, housewives with concentric pit stains under their blouses. Sometimes they sat on laps. Sometimes they lowered their pants, pulled their baggy kurtas like marquees over occasional lovers. Sometimes they rode many things at once—the 47A double-decker bus sardined with bodies, the undulating thighs of a chit-fund manager, boys with nostrils ringed in silver. They attended women's colleges owned by missionaries, by Franciscan nuns crusted over with virtue, by sisters mouthing livid hymns to Mother Mary of the Passion. Sometimes they sustained eye-contact with their married stalkers hovering around the lips of the bus—agriculture certification employees, Sanskrit teachers with unkempt hair, traffic policemen checkered in khaki and white. Sometimes they were pursued by an assortment of men who garlanded them with urgent obscenities, threats, desperate pleas, threats, promises of love, threats, marriage offers, threats. Girls who sat at the back of buses jostled through their lives with resolve, their elbows skimming iron railings, skin, their seats, yours. They wanted for nothing. Nothing that you or I could offer them, nothing at all.

M. L. Krishnan hails from the coastal shores of Tamil Nadu, India. She is a 2019 graduate of the Clarion West Writers' Workshop, and her work has appeared, or is forthcoming in *The Offing*, *trampset*, *Paper Darts*, *Sonora Review* and elsewhere. You can find more of her writing at mlkrishnan.com.

MOTHER-DAUGHTER

KATHRYN KULPA

The smell hits first. It always does. Diaper pail ammonia mixed with lion cage, meat and blood and wild. She slams her face against the bars. That's always the worst, not because they won't hold—they always do—but the heedlessness, the willingness to split a lip, to lose a tooth. To be ugly and torn, but free.

He steps back, judging the distance to the door.

She can't get out, I say.

It's one of her bad days. I shouldn't have invited him to dinner. I shouldn't have let him see her. But maybe it's better to give him an excuse to get away.

Has she always been, he starts, but doesn't finish. His Adam's apple bobs.

She was pretty once, I tell him. I look at the side table, the picture of us in matching daisy dresses she sewed herself. I was five then. I didn't know why she locked herself in every full moon. Didn't know why people crossed themselves when they passed our house.

It doesn't matter, he says. I still love you.

I won't always be pretty, I say.

And he says it doesn't matter, doesn't matter at all, and I wonder if that was what my father said, before. Was that what male praying mantises told themselves, or drone bees?

He says he'll break the curse. He says he'll save me. He says he has a silver bullet, blessed by the priest, and I say no, don't hurt her, and then I see the rifle pointed at me. I'm so sorry, he says, and then there's a roar I feel in my feet, the screech of metal and sheetrock crumbling in a rain of plaster dust and I was wrong about those bars and when I can see again she's licking the blood off her ghost-coated arm and thank you, I say, and she looks up and I can't tell if she hears or understands but I think she knows me even though she just keeps licking her arm because it's one of her bad days.

Kathryn Kulpa is a writer and editor with stories in *Atticus Review*, *Flash Frog*, *No Contact*, *trampset*, and *Wigleaf*. Her work was included in *Best Microfiction 2020* and *2021* and has been nominated for Best Small Fictions. She is senior flash editor at *Cleaver* magazine.

CALLA LILIES

TARA ISABEL ZAMBRANO

The girls speak of pantyhose and glitter, the girls go on about lace and liquor, the girls run, fall, rip their stockings, the girls get up, hay in their hair, specks of dirt on their cheeks, breathing the dirty, humid air of the East Side, the girls go on about their bruises, on their arms, on their thighs, some above their hearts, the girls knot their hands, the girls shake their booties to *All the Single Ladies* by Beyoncé, the girls stroke their hair when asked if they are sleeping with each other's boyfriends, *Seriously?* the girls say, rolling their eyes, *you're imagining things, just relax*, the girls slow-mouth, bird breathe, lean in, the girls ring like dull songs in the school hallways, the girls dress up in slinky skirts, pussyfoot and skip class to visit the West End where the houses are honey pink with interiors like Pottery Barn, the girls bump against men in dim lit bars, the girls smoke their cigars, the girls fuck them leaning against the wall or in their trucks shaking loose like the ground after the rain, and later, much later, the girls take a drag from the same cigarette, grasp, clutch each other's fingers, *No I'm fine*, the girls say, and crash curses as they flick ash, the girls a swarm of fireflies, pop their light fuses one by one until the cigarette is about done, a red, vanishing tail in the dirt, the girls turn off their sex, blowing white puffs in the small hours of the night until motor bikers with dirty hair and burning eyes stop by and the girls loosen their curls, the girls hope the men will buy them milkshakes and fries because the girls have been drinking beer and now their bodies are lit up with a hot pink hunger, the girls prance around the leathery chests, the girls rope in the dust from the revving engines, the girls bloom and blossom like calla lilies, flapping their arms in the air, their way of saying, saying, *Look at me, look at me!*

Tara Isabel Zambrano is a writer of color and the author of a full-length collection, *Death, Desire, And Other Destinations* by Okay Donkey Press.

HOW SKINNY CAN I GET

COREY ZELLER

The gum trees are exactly as they sound: pink and shining. A bud sprouts from your arm. Roots form like crosswords below the sidewalk, carrying away men in suits like magnets by their loafers. No other news to report.   The wallpaper drinks itself.   Telephone poles erect themselves out of dust.   And you: you're accused of being an island so you buy a posh apartment in the city and fill it with sand. When you walk down the street it seems someone keeps drawing you smaller and smaller, a living thing among endless sculpture.

Corey Zeller is the author of *Man Vs. Sky* (YesYes Books, 2013) and *You and Other Pieces* (Civil Coping Mechanisms, 2015). His work has appeared in various journals. He recently received his MFA from Syracuse University.

WHAT GRIEF IS

KINNESON LALOR

It's missing noises like the gentle tap of nails as you walk from room to room, just checking nothing has changed in case some space has opened up that needs your affection.

It's missing temperatures like the way your body gives heat, leaving warm shallow dents on anything soft.

It's missing fury because you opened the door just to taste the air.

It's also presence. Presence of things that are yours alone and I have no use for now, never before noticed sitting loud and mutely unused.

It's months later when I clean the drain to find parts of you weaving across the dark pipe with soap residue and knots of my hair. I won't want to throw you away so I'll leave the grey mass and the shower will flood and the boards outside the door will warp and they'll creak from that moment on and I'll blame you and hold on to that simple irritation long after a professional probes a camera in the hole and tells me I have a blockage.

"I know," I'll say, "but I need someone else to fix it."

And he'll tell me it's always easiest to prevent rather than cure and I'll think: "what a fucking poet." But when he draws away the last part of you and empties you under the cherry tree, I smell blossom even though it's only January, and I'm one image further from grief.

Kinneson Lalor is an Australian writer and mathematician who lives in the UK. She has both a PhD in Physics and an MSt in Creative Writing from the University of Cambridge. She loves her chickens and dog. Find her at www.kinnesonlalor.com.

WHAT I THINK KING KONG IS ABOUT (HAVING NEVER SEEN KING KONG)

KIRSTEN RENEAU

I think maybe King Kong is about the dangers of colonialism, about how people aren't supposed to be everywhere, how knowing your limitations is a virtue. I think maybe King Kong is about how cruelty always backfires and eventually animals will take over and it will be our own faults and then I realize I'm thinking of Planet of the Apes (which I've also never seen). I think maybe King Kong is about me, about how I've got an anger in my heart, about how I'd like to make all of New York (where I've never been) stand in awe of my enormousness, how I'd rather do that then try Weight Watchers again, try to make myself small and holdable again. Maybe it's about how women are supposed to fit into the palm of a hand or maybe it's about how I think I'd like to hold a woman in my hands and know she loves me back—despite my size, despite my rage, despite the fact that maybe we defy the laws of nature and possibly physics. I think maybe King Kong is about defiance in a way that is not necessarily proud, but demands to be seen. I think maybe King Kong is about looking things in the eyes. I think maybe King Kong is about how sad the gorillas in the zoo look when they are alone or maybe it's about how apes cannot cry, but sometimes they make a noise like weeping. I think maybe King Kong is about how not being understood can make anyone want to destroy something. How Washoe the chimp learned her captors' language to be heard. How she tried to cry when her baby died but couldn't make the tears come. I think maybe King Kong is about being enormously, climbing-the-empire-state-building, forcing witness, outstandingly

alone.

Kirsten Reneau received her MFA from the University of New Orleans. Her writing has been nominated for various awards, and even won some. Read more of her work at: www.kirsten-reneau.com.

EXCAVATING

ALEYNA RENTZ

We are chipping away at the moon. Women wear it on their fingers; their fiancés make jokes about George Bailey in *It's a Wonderful Life*, his prescient wish to lasso it and bring it home. Moon cufflinks hold lawyers and businessmen together. Bits of moon dangle from earlobes and clasp together handbags. My daughter waves at the sky, saying goodnight to the little men with pickaxes on the surface of the moon. Skinny and withered, beef jerky men—this is what she calls them. Sometimes she spots retired ones in parking lots, and I pull her away. Look, Mommy, she says, and I tell her it's not polite to point. We bought a piece to give her when she's older, a bit of moon hung on a twenty-four-karat gold chain. My idea, not my husband's. He's gone now. He left one night in tears, saying he couldn't stand a waveless ocean. I mean he leapt. That kind of gone. I should've known it would happen, should've paid more attention to the faraway look he got whenever my bracelet made ripples in his cereal milk. He was a man with no gravitational pull, who let himself be pulled instead. A tragedy, but what can you do?

My boyfriend says Mars will be next. He swears my ring will be red and glowing and teeming with microscopic life. The beef jerky men? my precious daughter asks. No, we tell her, not them. She wants to know what will happen when the moon is totally gone. It'll never be gone, my sweet, not for you. Hold up your necklace to the dark window and squint.

Aleyna Rentz is a writer from Southwest Georgia who now lives in Baltimore, MD. Her writing has appeared in *The Iowa Review*, *The Cincinnati Review*, *Glimmer Train*, *Pleiades*, and elsewhere. She currently serves as Senior Fiction Reader for *Salamander*.

UNDERAGE.

JESSICA JUNE ROWE

I watch my grandmother age backward. Black finds its way into her brittle grey ends and seeps upward, her hair growing fuller, hiding the speckled patches of her scalp. Her skin smooths and thickens; no more bruises and purple-pinched veins. She leaves indents in the armrests when she pushes out of her wheelchair. When the window won't open she breaks the glass with her IV stand. It's a four-story fall to the ground, but she pilots her hospital gown like a wingsuit, gliding down in slow, shrinking circles. She lands in a roll that turns into a crawl. It feels like it all happens in a blink; her hair is short again, dark wisps on her young head, and her hands and knees must be so soft, must be burning on the hot sidewalk. A woman walking out of the fertility clinic spots my grandmother, all alone in the hospital courtyard, and rushes over. She picks my grandmother up, wrapping her in the hospital gown turned wingsuit turned swaddling blanket. The woman looks around in confusion, left, right, then up. I pull away from the window. When no one appears, the woman holds her tighter and sniffs, inhaling the scent of her newborn skin, fighting off her own tears. It must tickle; my grandmother laughs. I'm still hidden out of sight, but through the broken glass I can still see her: a thousand fractal versions of her, the courtyard, the blanket, the hospital room, the woman, myself. I see the woman's confusion turn to wonder to determination and, after a moment of hesitation, she sprints toward the parking garage. I lean out back out the window to watch her run. From over the woman's shoulder, my grandmother takes her thumb out of her mouth to wave goodbye.

Jessica June Rowe is a writer, playwright, and perpetual daydreamer. She is Flash Fiction Editor of *Exposition Review*. Her own fiction has appeared in *Okay Donkey Magazine*, *Gigantic Sequins*, and *Pidgeonholes*, among others. She also really loves chai lattes. Find more of her work at willwriteforchai.com.

TAPEWORM

KRISTEN LOESCH

Mei knows she has tapeworms because she's felt them squirming, slithering, shimmying in her belly since she swam here from Shenzhen, or maybe it's just one long tapeworm longer than a fresh-water eel longer than the straw mat she sleeps on longer than the last smile her mother will ever give her, but that smile was before she started swimming, and she thought she was swimming only from the new Communist China into Hong Kong she thought she was swimming only four kilometres but the truth nobody told her is that you will still be swimming even after you crawl up on those docks drenched down to your bone marrow you will still be swimming when you find a place to stay in a sooty shanty town that clings to the edge of Kowloon by the fingertips you will still be swimming when your own fingertips are bloodied from picking over rags for cotton waste, six days of work for a pound of cotton, because the truth nobody tells you is that you are trapped in somebody's bowels and you will never stop swimming, swimming, swimming and whenever Mei thinks of that, she feels a little sorry for her tapeworms and doesn't tell anyone for just one more day.

Kristen Loesch grew up in San Francisco. She is an award-winning writer of short fiction. Her debut historical novel, *The Porcelain Doll*, is out in the UK from Allison & Busby (February 2022) and forthcoming in the US from Berkley (Spring 2023).

AFTER THE THRILL

AMY LYONS

The woman took herself to the amusement park instead of the motel. The man she'd met at the hardware store had ended it a week ago. In fantasies, her soft-spoken husband pounded the door of room six. Caught, she loved him again.

The woman had never ridden a rollercoaster alone. A muscled arm sleeved in tattoos jerked her lap-bar. Did it ever unhinge? Hers could be the first. Evening news would outline her ejection at the second hairpin, feature the photo from yearbook, *most likely to...* what? She couldn't recall. "Alone," the reporter would make her voice grave, "in the middle of Wednesday." They'd broadcast B-roll of a famed coaster's hill, a longshot of the cart's ticking ascent cut hard at the drop to unspooling track. TV audiences would white-knuckle couch cushions, grasp easy-chair arms, the point-of-view shift leaning them in.

"Weight distribution," the Ferris wheel operator said, suggesting the woman join a father and son. The son head-locked a stuffed tiger and hid, suspicious of the woman's smoky eyeshadow, her greying roots. The father smiled an apology, lay a hand on the son's half-buried head. Wanting the best for all parties involved, the woman stepped aside and a doe-legged teen sprang into the space, followed by her heavyset friend, who bore no shame in accepting a boost from the balding operator. They rose. Something like a confession welled up in the woman's throat. When the umbrellaed cart drifted back down, the girl whose body refused easy containment channeled the tiger's cheerful voice, climbed the big cat up the boy's arm, roared it into his ear. The boy's stuttering laughter dispersed into sky.

She whacked moles, hurled softballs at milk bottles rigged not to topple, joined a water-gun firing squad to shoot wooden clowns in their glory-hole smiles. Nothing unnumbed her. A cotton candy bouffant, a cross-hatched funnel cake dredged in old snow, a skewered corn dog reeking of oil. She chewed and swallowed and smacked, but could not make her body feel sated or sick.

Pinned to the wall as the Gravitron spun, she welcomed the pressure. One at a time, she unstuck her limbs and let the wind slam them back to her sides. She looked down just in time to see the floor fall away. She contorted her face into a smile at the sight of her dangling feet. Unseen forces held her aloft.

Amy Lyons has stories in or forthcoming from *BULL*, *FRiGG*, *HAD*, *Waxwing*, *Prime Number*, *No Contact*, *(mac)ro(mic)*, *Versification*, *Literary Mama*, *Lunch Ticket*, *100 Word Story*, *Flash Frog*, *Anti-Heroin Chic*, and *The Daily Drunk*. She's an alum of Bennington's MFA, the Millay Colony, and Tin House's summer workshop.

TEN AMAZING FACTS ABOUT THE HUMAN BODY

JOANNA THEISS

A teenager has two hundred and six bones, ninety-four less than she had when she was born.

If you stretched her blood vessels from end to end and joined them together, you could loop the filament over the moon, twice.

In a single year, she produces enough saliva to fill two bathtubs.

If you counted her heartbeat for just twelve minutes, the number of beats would exceed the student body of our elementary school, where a rabbit-faced boy once twisted an inky bruise into my cheek.

It took less time than it takes for blood to travel from my heart through my entire body for you to tell the principal what the boy had done, and less time than it takes for the blood to travel back to my heart for you to demand justice.

The human tongue contains three thousand taste buds, equivalent to the number of miles between our house and your college, which I measured by studying a photo album jammed with pictures of us, your arm looped around my shoulders, me wearing a dress that had been your favorite.

There are fourteen bones in the human face, my age in years when our brother snuck into my bedroom, knowing that you were too far away to help me.

Sisters share fifty percent of their DNA. That percentage doesn't change when sisters split apart like cells, when they continue to divide until the tissue is crowded with voices that say I must be lying, accusing our brother to get attention, when what I crave is not attention, but for you to hold my hand as my tears fill bathtubs, as the weight of my shame collapses my lungs, as I burn in the eighty-six billion nerve cells of my brain.

The human mouth can make eight hundred individual sounds. Ninety-nine percent more than it takes to say, "I believe you."

Joanna Theiss (she/her) is a lawyer turned writer living in Washington, DC. Her publication credits include articles in literary and academic journals and popular magazines. Her website (www.joannatheiss.com) features links to short stories, flash fiction, book reviews, and interesting collages.

RIDING BIKES WITHOUT TRAINING WHEELS

JENNIFER TODHUNTER

The summer we divorce, the annual Perseid shower peaks on your birthday, and I lay in my yard, my clothing damp with dew, stare up at the sky the way we did that time we went camping on the island, that time our boys attached glow-in-the-dark bracelets to the bikes we'd just removed their training wheels from, and they hooted as they rode through the darkness avoiding fire pits and tent lines, and that girl who'd asked her boyfriend to marry her on the bank of the river a few hours earlier was all smiles and gentle touches with him, and he was all sweet words and infatuation with her, and they bought you a four-pack of Guinness as a gift and we sat in tattered camping chairs for hours, our necks craned back, our eyes searching the sky, waiting and waiting and waiting, and the newly-engaged girl caught the shift of the stars with her fancy camera when they shot through the night and it blew my mind to see tracers like that, the journey, the inevitable extinguishment, and none of us spoke except to announce another, *another one*, we'd say, *did you see it*, or, *that was a fast one, a bright one, a large one*, and I'd never seen a shooting star before that night, never seen something streak through the sky except a plane or a bird or a firework, and while I didn't see a shooting star that summer we divorced, I did catch one that night we camped when I walked to the outhouse alone on a trail leading to the beach, and I stood in awe of its beauty, of its momentum, of its ability to shoot through the galaxy on its own, unattached and unadorned.

FRIDAYS

JENNIFER TODHUNTER

We'd skip school on Fridays, joke that Fridays were for getting fried, and we'd zip through the small town streets in our friend's green 510, her muffler hanging on by its fingernails, her stereo cranking the Pixies or RATM, and we'd take turns rolling joints in the cracked spines of our textbooks, hotbox the car with our shared exhales, and it must've looked like we were emerging from the backstage of some shitty singing competition, all smoke and frazzle falling into the fresh air when we finally reached the beach at the bottom of Beacon Avenue, and we'd climb down the cliffs to the shore, lie on beds of kelp, and we'd rip off pieces and stuff them into our pasty mouths, laugh when we heard the inevitable crunch of sand between our teeth, all of us thinking how the softness of the seaweed sort of resembled the tongue of the last guy's face we sucked, and on hot days, we'd shed our shirts, lie topless in the scorch of the sun and burn our tits and stomachs, places we were dying for that guy to run his fingers over again, maybe dipping lower, pressing harder this time, and we'd zone out on the eagles sitting in the trees lining the cliff, watch them teach their eaglets how to fly, watch them surf the tide of the wind alongside each other, and we'd wonder what that must feel like, to jump out of a nest and know there was only so far you could fall before someone else would catch you.

Jennifer Todhunter's stories have appeared in *The Forge*, *Hobart*, *Monkeybicycle*, and elsewhere. Her work has been selected for *Best Small Fictions*, *Best Microfiction* and *Wigleaf's* Top 50 Very Short Fictions. She is the Editor-in-Chief of *Pidgeonholes* and founder of *Trash Mag*. Find her at www.foxbane.ca or @JenTod_.

DON'T GET LOST IN THE DINOSAUR KINGDOM

CORTNEY PHILLIPS MERIWETHER

After driving by billboards proclaiming WALK AMONGST THE DINOSAURS and LAST CHANCE FOR PREHISTORIC FUN for miles, you looked at me and said, "Well, we were going to stop to pee soon anyway," so you veered right off the exit before I could say anything, stood vigil outside the women's bathroom while I went in, then led me by the hand toward the arrowed path into the woods—and, look, I know I shouldn't have felt scared, and obviously they were just fiberglass dinosaurs, but they were also really fucking big fiberglass dinosaurs, and some of them were practically camouflaged among the trees, so I didn't even notice them until they were *right there*—but the point is, it was one thing to laugh the first time I jumped, because maybe I could have laughed that off too, but you saying, "Jesus, Molly, this is a roadside exhibit geared toward fucking six-year-olds" when I started to cry really didn't help, and maybe I wasn't crying about the pink pastel triceratops or the pale green brontosaurus or even the twenty bucks you took from me for our tickets—maybe I was crying about how we were 1,500 miles into this cross-country move and I still couldn't forget the shake in my mother's voice when she said *this is a mistake you can still get out I can help you* as I followed you out the door, because now with each step down this ridiculously marked path in the woods, I was becoming less and less sure about you being the only person I knew for miles—and even worse about you being the only person who knew me.

Cortney Phillips Meriwether is a writer and editor living in Charlottesville, Virginia with her husband and two sons. Her work has been published by *Ninth Letter*, *Wigleaf*, *matchbook*, *CHEAP POP*, *Monkeybicycle*, and others.

LEFT TO THEIR OWN DEVICES, THEY BECAME THEM

MICHELLE MOROUSE

Jinny blamed herself at first. She'd skipped Junior's basketball games to go to spin class and begged off her mom's church tea. She guzzled wine at her book club when she could have cuddled up with her husband to watch superheroes save the universe. Buff men in tights—would it have been so awful?

Ultimately, though, Jinny knew she couldn't have changed the outcome. She cooked dinner most nights, but her family barely looked up from their devices at the table. Her family squandered countless hours, hunched over phones, tablets, laptops, barely stopping to eat, or go to the bathroom. (Mom wet her pants once.)

Her husband fell asleep in his La-Z-Boy chair each evening. One morning, Jinny woke to find him gone. A dented PC rested on his chair. Then her mother became a purse-friendly teal tablet, her son a game console.

Hoping to salvage some connection, Jinny went on

the devices, to no avail. Hubby's PC was stalled in a crocheting chat room, Junior's console displayed neon curlicues, and Mom's tablet featured people in Disney costumes... enjoying each other's company. An Abandonee support group helped at first, but soon the others spent most of the session on their phones, then they stopped showing up.

She drove the devices around occasionally, set a place for everyone at holidays. It wasn't so bad—they'd been gone before they were gone. There was no snipping over who drank the most, no wincing while her husband hacked at the turkey, no holding her breath when her fumble prone mother insisted on washing the good china.

Jinny re-opened her taxidermy shop. She fills her free time with scuba lessons, paperbacks from the used bookstore, volunteering at the soup kitchen. Each night, she climbs the stairs and pauses a moment, before plugging everyone in.

Michelle Morouse is a Detroit area pediatrician. Her flash fiction and poetry has appeared recently in *Unbroken, Litro Online, The Citron Review, Ponder Review, Necessary Fiction, Wigleaf, Peregrine, Lullwater Review, The MacGuffin, Pembroke Magazine*, and *Cease, Cows*. She serves on the board of Detroit Working Writers.

YEARS

DIANE PAYNE

For weeks, I hauled Claudia, the old cat, outside for a bit of air, putting her on my lap while we sat on the front steps listening to music in the evenings, or wrapping her in a blanket placed in her cat bed on a lawn chair during the day, sometimes setting her on the ground where she seemed much happier in the grass, which made me worry that she seemed almost too content, dragging her hind legs into the overgrown ivy to find that perfect spot, and I'd think, oh no, not yet, assuring her I was making buttery white fish for dinner, then mumble stories about Greece, and how the cats came up to empty chairs at restaurants, and she'd give me a how tacky look bringing up Greece while the vet says she'll be dead soon. I changed our routine and stuffed her in a pouch to carry on a walk, while the neighbors looked at Claudia with pity, and at me as if I was a lunatic. At home in the backyard, where the neighbor kids climbed on top of their swing set yelling hi over and over, the dog and I watched Claudia fade away. And then, without much fanfare, I placed her in the hole I had dug in the ivy earlier in the day, realizing that I have spent more years living with Claudia than I did with my own mother, and I have no idea why this realization occurs while burying my old cat, but nothing makes sense in the end.

Diane Payne spends a lot of time taking walks and swimming. Her most recent publications include: *Abandon Journal*, *Cutleaf*, *Another Chicago Magazine*, *Whale Road Review*, *Pine Hills Review*, *Tiny Spoon*, *Ellipsis Zine*, *Bending Genres*, and *The New York Times*.

INHERITANCE

GRACE Q. SONG

All day I've been angry in upstate New York. Somewhere in the Catskills, my father and I sit in a small white fishing boat, encircled by red cedars and feasted on by mosquitoes. By the edge of the lake, a family of swans search for waterweed and muskgrass. The pair come every summer to breed, and my family came every summer until whatever line that wound my parents together unraveled, and my father left without taking a single thing. Now, a year later, the man in front of me, who once fished gold-foil chocolates and miracles from my ears and placed them as a promise in my hands, has a girlfriend and a shiny new job in the city. He doesn't mention my arms, crossed like a gate, the way I only answer his questions and never ask him any. He just says *look*, pulls the line above the shoulder of purple mountains, across a cloudless palm of blue, the hook glinting like a silver eye. When it falls and murmurs against the water, the lake gasps open.

Grace Q. Song is a Chinese American writer. Her poetry and fiction have been published in *SmokeLong Quarterly*, *PANK*, *THRUSH*, *The Journal*, *The Cincinnati Review*, and elsewhere. Previous works have been selected for inclusion in *Best Microfiction*, *Best Small Fictions*, and *Best of the Net*. She attends Columbia University.

FREEZING POINT

STAR SU

His previous girlfriends were slender wicks, all smoke and candied wax. And when he smoothed the hair from your face, you believed that you could be a candle too, hemmed in safe by the darkness.

He watches you make new bones. Complimented you for it, hand warm between your shoulder blades, now sharp little things. Steak for the lady too. Watches you become a knife between his fingers. You like this new mold for the first time, because it was designed not by you or your mother.

He brings you sauvignon blanc, but it has frozen in the backseat. Holds your wrists when you try to sift through the glass, spinning in the thawed wine. *Aren't you afraid of anything?* You bring your lips to the bowl and swallow.

After he falls asleep, you take his keys, leather cuff still warm from his back pocket. The moon is glossed over. The snow falls in clumps, but the ground is still warm, the landscape unchanged. Your sweaters wear on, muffled in the dryer. Heels slumped in the foyer. You think of leaving a note, but your hands are too weightless to hold anything down.

You don't know what he dreams of, only that he likes to pull you to his chest. Sometimes, you like to drown a little that way listening to his murmurs of someone else's name. It is a game you like to play in the morning, asking for his dreams. It is not really a game, because every time he lies, you believe him.

But now you have the night between you, your breath forming ribbons of vapor. Snow surges against the windows, and you click the buttons he showed you to melt everything. You press them out of sequence, because this could still be a dream and doing something wrong will still wake you up. Instead, the snowflakes lose their angles, slide into thin streams. As you pass silos and mall pavilions, they collect in pockets but they are no match for the laws of temperature. When the molecules go cracking and spitting back into ice, you brace yourself. You should have known that nothing changes form so easily, not even the water that floods you now.

Star Su is an engineer and writer living in Brooklyn. Her fiction appears or is forthcoming in *The Offing*, *Black Warrior Review*, *Porter House Review*, and elsewhere. Find them online at starcsu.com.

I DO NOT WANT TO LIVE WITHOUT YOU

CATHY ULRICH

The motel with its raggedy bedspread and tottering TV that only plays 17 channels, two of them Spanish, and a swimming pool near the parking lot all concrete deck and *swim at your own risk* and we are swimming at our own risk, broken pool heater and all, chattering teeth when we come out onto the sun-warmed ground, and maybe later there will be consequences and police cars, maybe later it will be like our parents said, but now it is us dangling our feet in cold water and sucking on dripping grape popsicles we got from the little store down the street and our shoulders going brown, brown, brown in the sun and the sound of the TV through our open motel window, *No quiero vivir sin ti.*

Cathy Ulrich is the founding editor of *Milk Candy Review*, a journal of flash fiction. She lives in Montana with her daughter and only one small animal. Her work has appeared in various journals and anthologies.

STAR SWALLOWED

OLIVIA WOLFORD

Her white dress was the only detail that stayed consistent in the retellings, how it shone in the dazzle that poured down. Most said her dog Cricket was taken up with her, though others claimed he still frisked the edges of their fields, pissing off barn cats. Either way it was agreed he was an inky, yippy little thing, one they preferred out of sight. Come to think of it, they preferred her out of sight too; she'd been a hazy child, more curtain of water than girl. Her brothers wouldn't speak for seven months after, and they weren't boys of many words to begin with. "She was swallowed," one had confided, "by stars." Truth was, they'd both been bowled clean over by the dazzle, witnesses only to the insides of their eyelids. It was said the cows minded their business while she was taken up. The horses, of course, watched the whole thing. They saw her bathed in moonbeam certainty, head upturned, swimming with clean strokes to a place beyond all light.

Olivia Wolford is a writer, educator, and anthropologist from Dallas, Texas.

YOU WILL NEVER NEED TO WALK AGAIN

YUNYA YANG

With a strip of long, cream-colored cloth, her feet are wrapped, toes crushed, joints snapped. Tighter and narrower, the bind gains with each passing day, her pain boils and burns. At night, she lies unsleeping, unseeing, biting down at the crook of her thumb and pressing her purple feet against the soothing, chilling wall. Poets sing the beauty of small feet, curved as the crescent moon, delicate like a golden lotus floating on a pond. How lovely she walks in those pointed, embroidered little shoes! She imagines that Cinderella bound her own feet, bamboo chips to sculpt the shape, porcelain shards to cut the bone, peony powder to cover the sweet, rotten smell, the betraying blood seeping from her wounds. As she descends the grand stairs, her body sways with each step like the sickly branches of a willow tree, and with each step the pain streaks through her, before she crumbles on the palm of a prince.

Yunya Yang was born and raised in Central China and moved to the US when she was eighteen. Her work appears in *Gulf Coast*, *Hobart*, *Split Lip Magazine*, among others. Find her at yunyayang.com and on Twitter @YangYunya.

CONTINGENCIES

SUSAN PERABO

This is what you do if he wakes up sad. This is what you do if he comes home angry. This is what you do if he stops taking his medication. This is what you do if he stays awake until sunrise. This is what you do if he won't text you back. This is what you do if he yells at you in the driveway. This is what you do if the neighbors look over from their porch. This is what you do if he's grieving his father. This is what you do if he recoils when you touch his shoulder. This is what you do if he suddenly seems fine. This is what you do if he opens the car door while you're driving. This is what you do if he says you're a liar. This is what you do if he breaks the vase your sister made for you. This is what you do if he suddenly seems fine. This is what you do if he says his heart is racing. This is what you do if he rages while you're holding the baby. This is what you do if he rages while he's holding the baby. This is what you do if the car is gone. This is what you do if he's had three beers. This is what you do if he's had eight beers. This is what you do if he says he's a monster. This is what you do if he says you made him into a monster. This is what you do if he asks you to lie for him. This is what you do if your sister says she wants to come for a visit. This is what you do if he suddenly seems fine. This is what you do if you can't find the car keys. This is what you do if he tells you he should kill himself. This is what you do if he tells you he might kill himself. This is what you do if he locks you out of the house. This is what you do if he locks you out of the house with the baby inside. This is what you do if he says he's sorry. This is what you do. This is what you do. This is what you do.

Susan Perabo's most recent books are *The Fall of Lisa Bellow* (2017) and *Why They Run the Way They Do* (2016). Her fiction has been anthologized in *The Best American Short Stories*, *Pushcart Prize Stories*, and *New Stories from the South*. She is a professor of creative writing at Dickinson College.

ALL THE THINGS THEY COULDN'T HAND BACK

EMMA PHILLIPS

He left his heart in Kowloon. She'd asked him to stay, but his wages were paid by the British, who had given him a bonus and transferred him to Dubai. She looked for his heart on the Star Ferry, felt the butterfly wings of its beat in her footsteps, held out her hands in Temple Street Market, hoping a vendor might drop it in them. A heart is slippery, like lychees.

She wondered if he'd stashed his heart on the tram, under the seat where he'd first held her hand. That way, when she grew tired of independence or of slurping noodles staring at nothing but her own reflection, she could find it again. He'd said he would visit, but she was not sure if the handover of power meant return tickets. Perhaps his heart was watching her from The Peak, on the spot where they had learned to admire the city.

A heart was a strange thing to leave behind. If she'd been the one who'd had to go, she would've been more practical, left him something useful like a compass or a Rolex.

Her apartment seemed smaller somehow, first July circled red on her calendar. She quit her English classes and dreamed in Cantonese again. His heart kept beating. Sometimes she heard it thump inside the walls.

When she stopped searching, the heart started to follow her. She felt it dripping in the rainy season, heard it echo in a stairwell, sensed it squeeze between her and a friend at the cinema. It was fatter and uglier than she remembered. His heart became an inconvenience, like a stray piece of tissue caught on a shoe. She wore ear plugs and tried to ignore it.

In the end, she had to remove it. When she finally scooped it into her hands, it wasn't as heavy as she had thought it would be. She took a moment to study its mass, the pulp of its surface, shiny and bloody. If she wanted to, she could squeeze it until it burst like a melon. That would be messy. She wrestled his heart into a bag, taped it shut, and threw it as far as she could into the harbor.

Emma Phillips lives in rural Devon with her husband, son and two guinea pigs. She discovered flash fiction during lockdown and is now hooked. She won second place in the 18th Bath Flash Fiction Award and her work has been published by *Mslexia*, *Blink-Ink*, *Flash Fiction Magazine* and *Popshot*.

NONE OF US

BECCA YENSER

We pick the black crusted grease off the cheeseburgers. We look at the sky. We hunger for home. We watch the river, where there is a goose with netting wrapped around her wings. The netting is probably lawn netting because the earth around here is sliding into the river. We see a different goose, a crying goose, swimming in circles. We say nothing. We pull at our cheeseburger wrappers and wait for our tongues to numb to the salt. We pray but we pray separately, in our own separate ways. We wish things would've gone different. We make excuses then discard them, stumble along the green netting buried in the earth. We pass the tree where a homeless man leaned against and died. *Drug overdose*, the cop had said. But we have a different grief. We have grief that we sprinkle on our food at night. Grief that smudges itself on the bathroom mirror, trickles black down the drain from our charcoal toothpaste, gurgles in the toilet after we flush. Our grief needs us to remain vigilant to it, so we are. We say some words that seem light, normal, cheerful: *the stars look so, the bridge lights are, the air sure is.*

We see our neighbors walking with their golden-haired child in the sunshine. The ground here is full of burrs that will stick to your socks and make you cry. The little girl, we notice, does not go barefoot in the grass but is bundled up, carried, ears like pink buds escaping her hat. We wipe our eyes with the edges of our mittens. We don't look back. We wipe the mud from our hands. We wipe the blood on our jeans. We count the days we have gone without her. We imagine the empty shadowy womb, sullen as a plain rock wall. Refusing to give, refusing to grow, refusing to be photogenic, or anything to smile at.

Becca Yenser is the author of the poetry collection *Too High and Too Blue In New Mexico* (Dancing Girl Press) and the creative nonfiction flash collection, *The Grief Lottery* (ELJ Editions, December 2021). Their work appears in *Hobart*, *Heavy Feather Review*, *Madcap Review*, *Fanzine*, and elsewhere.

SALVAGE

LACEY YONG

She's searching the ship—peering around plastic algae tubes, rifling through the detritus of other people's lives so she can furnish her own—when her flashlight plucks out a floating figure, fetal in the dark.

A corpse?

Never mind. It's not what she is seeking. Best to grab whatever she can find and go. Since leaving Earth, she has learned that shoring up her indifference is the only way to deal with bodies that hang forgotten in space like so much trash.

Beneath the figure's helmet, a mouth contorts, and her grip on the flashlight wavers.

Leave it, she tells herself, even as she drifts closer.

It's a child. A boy, perhaps, though the spacesuit makes it hard to tell for sure. She draws nearer and his eyes bulge and his bluish lips part to expose stubby yellow teeth; against his visor, his breath pulses white like spray. She can almost hear his gasps, the tortured whine of his lungs searching for oxygen.

"Mama whales lift their young to the surface to breathe," Ma once said. Beside their boat, the blowhole erupted, showering them in warm, sun-touched brine.

The ocean had been alive then.

So had Ma.

Lowering her flashlight, she fishes for her spare O2 bottle and shoves it into the boy's suit. When she was twelve, Ma had snuck her into the local aquarium and taught her how to use a baby bottle to feed a small beluga whale. Its black walnut eye had stared at her. It had been orphaned and was among the last of its kind.

The boy's chin jerks, his cracked lips stretching into a surprised "O" at the injection of fresh oxygen. She watches his exhalations and waits for the seconds to lengthen between each cloud of breath before gathering him in her arms and pushing off the metal deck.

As they surface into the black, their helmets touch, and his breathing rushes into her ears.

He is crying.

Angling their bodies towards her waiting shuttle, she rests her helmet against his as if their foreheads could touch, and when she does, his sobs ripple through her, eddying across her skin like small whirlpools on the water before the waves part and reveal the whale hidden beneath.

Lacey Yong is an emerging Chinese-Canadian writer. Her creative nonfiction has received multiple nominations for Best of the Net, and she is working on her first YA steampunk novel. She lives in Calgary with her husband and a baby on the way. "Salvage" is her first microfiction publication.

TOKYO PEARL

TERESA PLANA

I've got Grandma's hands, long and thick-veined, fingers knotty like redwood, stuffed in the back of my underwear drawer. Every morning I look at her prong-set ring, her nails pearly like an oil spill. When I pull out my least favorite bra, it is covered in fish scales of her chipped polish.

Mom visits on Sundays. After pancake lunch and Gin Rummy, we take turns putting the hands on. We press them lightly to our cheeks. We pat each other's tilted heads. We say words the hands never heard. Come here, honey. Such a beautiful, beautiful girl.

Teresa Plana is an aid worker based in Paris, where she thinks about books, croissants and humanitarian aid. Her work has appeared in *Hobart*, *Gulf Stream Magazine* and *PRISM international*. She is a reader for *Uncharted Magazine*. Find her on Twitter @malaidea.

ALLSORTS

SARAH SALWAY

The shopkeeper saves the best liquorice for him, taking out the torpedoes and adding more rosettes. Sometimes he comes in late, just when she's given up hope, and she'll still pretend to measure it out, weighing it carefully, adding a little more just so she can see his smile. He's so often grey with tiredness. Once, only once, she leant across the counter to wipe a mark off his face before she realised it was a thin scar, etched in so deep she was rubbing its shadow. He caught her hand, lifted it as gently as if it was some injured bird he was offering back to her. And every day they carry on this dance, not caring they are visible through the shop window. She spins the paper bag until it twists itself shut. And he counts out the coins as if each one is precious. And you and I watch them from the street, surrounded by so much sweetness. And you tell me you'd take down every jar on every shelf to fill my pockets with coconut mushrooms, wine gums, fruit salads. I say I'd swap it all for the one jelly baby. And *shhh*, you say, *he's about to go*. And her smile is so thin it matches the scar she'll never be able to rub off.

And he nods, pausing as if he's finally about to say something. And we both realise we are holding our breath. And we can't bear to look back at her after the shop door twinkles shut behind him. And so instead we hold hands to watch how he shuffles home, carrying his pink and white striped bag as if it weighs nothing at all.

Sarah Salway is a poet, novelist and short story writer based in Kent, England. She edits the Everyday Words newsletter. www.sarahsalway.co.uk.

HIP DEEP IN THE CHESAPEAKE

KAT LEWIS

It's our job to watch the crabs while Scooter kills them. On the dock of Port Isobel, it is late afternoon. Or maybe early evening. We can't be sure; they took our phones and iPods—anything with a clock—when we got off the boat. Welcome to Port Isobel, they said, leading us to the house where we're not allowed to flush the toilet. It's been three days of dock showers and trust fall bullshit. Now, we still don't know what time it is; all we know is that we are hungry, and there are forty crabs in buckets, their claws morse coding last words to each other. Don't let them out, Scooter said. We beat the crabs back with yard sticks and sniff our noses at crisp breezes. It is early September, and the bite of autumn is in the air, the temperature like the stale breath of heat—something that won't linger, something we'll miss. The other side of the island swallows the sunlight. Beyond the crabs and their buckets, beyond the docks and their showers, beyond the house where we can only flush shit, we see the sun through the trees, staccato like a flip book. The tick-tick of crab legs on plastic brings us back to the algae-tinged dock and the wisps of Spartina grass stretching towards us. Scooter's hand's inside a crab now. Light leaves a gilded frame around the writhing legs. Merciful, like a caress, he twists out the gills; its legs rag doll at its side. We are thirteen. It's our first time seeing something die.

물귀신 | MUL GWISHIN

KAT LEWIS

Noh Eunbi dies in a ditch in Delaware, and you will see her ghost. Miles away, on the Incheon bridge, under twin typhoons like twisting gears over the Korean peninsula, you will see her in a dress red as a bloodstain. Through your windshield's spray of angry rain and whipping wipers, you will see her waterlogged skin, see her broken neck, see her mouth—like the yawning maw of a deadman—open:

Dowa juseyo.

In this howl, you will know the name of your shame.

Noh Eunbi dies in a ditch in Delaware, miles away from the boarding school where you become addicted to an addict. In abandoned barns behind campus, watch her tongue curl around the words of your second language. Match your tongue to hers. On dorm room floors, form the rieul in your mouth for words like byul, bul, saramdeul. Stencil out each other's bodies with fingers light as breath. Love constellations of rug burns into the skin, and connect them with hands like salves. On nights like your birthday, use those hands to scrape vomit out of her mouth. When her nose bleeds like a fresh wound, hold a tissue to that small face and pretend to forget the hiding place for powders and pills. In the middle of the night, press your phone to your ear to hear the news, and watch your guilt manifest itself across the room like a black-robed god.

On that bridge to Seoul, remember when she taught you the word for water, the word for ghost. Put them together now. Amid rain and squall, you will meet her mul gwishin, but leave her there, pass through her ghost, watch the wraith of her dissipate like the cigarette smoke when she taught you how to eat yourself alive.

Kat Lewis graduated from Johns Hopkins University where she held the Saul Zaentz Fellowship. She received her MFA from the University of South Florida. Her work has appeared in *TriQuarterly, The Florida Review, Khôra*, and *The Rumpus*. In 2018, she was a Fulbright Creative Arts grantee in South Korea.

A TRAGIC MISSTEP IN EVOLUTION

MARVIN SHACKELFORD

One day they'll dig me from the limestone and ash so long settled around my frame and wonder what to do with me. The scene should be instructive: primitive homo-whatever we're called by then, -sapient long since come and gone and forgotten, simply laid down and died circa late-Holocene mass-extinction event. Perfectly preserved but totally useless. As he no doubt was in life, someone will joke. They laugh. Their laughter is a reedy, piping wind. Birdlike, slender and noncommittal and all I hate to think of being. They peck and scratch at the earth with diamond and light for what they were, grow disappointed and quickly learn to hide it. Look how wide! The brow a cavernous overhang, proboscis practically nonexistent. How did they call to the face of God? How did they rise into the heavens, bring forth the sun, reach into the waves of the universe's nectar or even just settle gently against their mates at night?

They won't appreciate, will lack a dating or DNA test to determine, how often I asked all that myself.

I ask it driving to the gas station for breakfast in the morning, no seatbelt on, think about it crossing the four-lane and back again with all the world bearing down heavy and hurried on me: Our God of endless wings and bloody skies doesn't even need a car wreck, a drunk rolling over the center line or an ambushing bridge abutment. He could take me sitting at the stop sign, choking on my food, later in my sleep. A heart attack while exercising. A tiny metal manmade meteorite dropped from orbit at just the right angle and moment. Something larger and undiscriminating, less aim but greater mass, enough to lower the clouds and leave only the lightest and longest-necked alive. There's no escape, no sneaking by we'd recognize. I'm thirsty. The sea leaves me high and dry. I keep a foot in the end of this human line, but up ahead I catch a glimpse of endless scrawny children breathing in the worst of me. They pick deep in the bones and stretch the treasure out carefully. There's nothing to do for it. That's all they have left to learn.

Marvin Shackelford is the author of *Tall Tales from the Ladies' Auxiliary* (stories, Alternating Current), *Endless Building* (poems) and the forthcoming *Field Guide to Lonely Birds* (flash, Red Bird Chapbooks). He resides, quietly, in Southern Middle Tennessee.

THE WOMAN WHO CUTS MY HAIR SAYS SHE'S BEEN HEARING NOISES IN HER APARTMENT

LESLIE WALKER TRAHAN

What kind of noises? I ask. Regular noises, she says, like the sound of someone living. Coffee brewing, water running, a cat purring. There are many explanations for what might be happening, but the woman who cuts my hair believes the door to another universe has cracked open in her apartment. She believes the noises she is hearing are sounds from a different life. Her life. A life where she drinks coffee and has a cat. She unhooks the frock covering my body and dusts it off while I look in the mirror. I think about telling her that when I was twelve I followed a set of footprints in the fresh snow outside our house until they disappeared in the middle of the street, and I wondered then if it wasn't something like that. But I don't. I slide my credit card into the little white square, and she gives me a slip of paper with a date three months into the future. I drive home. For dinner, there is frozen lasagna, red wine. I turn on the TV while I eat, and a show I used to watch when I was a child is on. It's the episode where the family dog disappears. The parents go to the pound and get a new dog that looks like the old one, but the old one has already found his way home. The kids are inside the house with their lost dog, and the parents are walking up to the front door with the new dog, the fake dog, and they open the door.

WHERE THERE'S SMOKE

LESLIE WALKER TRAHAN

I never saw my mother with a cigarette when she was alive, but now that she's dead, she goes through a pack a day at least. I smell her smoke in every room of my house. I find her butts smashed into my floors. She's with me while I make dinner. I grease the pan with butter. I prepare the chicken to roast. Then I hear the quick tick of a lighter, and when I turn around, there are ashes lining my pan. *Mother*, I say, *stop it*. But she never listens. She's already burned three holes in her recipe book, one in her wedding dress, too. At night, she waits for my husband to fall asleep before she starts in. There is the smell of smoke and the glimmer of a cigarette in the dark, and when I run my hands over my husband's chest, ashes grind against my palm. When I go out, I smell smoke on the streets. At the dry cleaner, the bank, the grocery store. Everyone breathes out smoke, long wispy curls that dissolve when I look straight at them. So many people, I think. So many secrets. I remember those final days. My mother in her thick floral nightgown, tucked tight beneath her sheets, and me leaning down to hear her better. *I sure would like to get in trouble someday*. Her lips were pinched back, her pale pink gums exposed. I stop at a bar and ask a man out front for a book of matches. He winks and drops one into my palm. *Come see us sometime, sweetheart*. I hear Mother's laugh behind me. When I turn, her embers graze my hand.

Leslie Walker Trahan is a writer from Austin, TX. Her work has appeared in *New Delta Review*, *Quarterly West*, *Passages North*, and *SmokeLong Quarterly*, among other publications. You can find her online at lesliewtrahan.com.

SEA MONSTERS

SUSAN TRIEMERT

Next year when we find out Dad has moved in with his "twin family", our late afternoon picnic will be recalled as if we're watching it through the breath of a campfire. The fiery fumes tilt and blur that shoreline air. Damp, with salt-twisted hair, we pile onto a yard sale blanket. Huddled together to block out wayward wind and swept-up sand, we nibble on saltines. Soon enough that briny breeze will help lick away our tears. But, for now, when Dad lays his spongy curls on Mom's lap, she kisses his forehead and calls him a sea monster.

Susan Triemert's collection of twenty-six essays on adoption, grief, and her mental health journey, *Guess What's Different*, will be published by Malarkey Books in May of 2022. Her website is susantriemert.com. A wife and mother of two sons, she lives in St. Paul, Minnesota.

THE TASTE OF OUR PAGES

SAGAN YEE

When the Deselit made first contact, they ate books. It was an honest mistake. We wanted to show them a place that represented our knowledge and culture. The Deselit thought we were offering them a snack. They chewed their way through half the YA section before our translators could intervene.

The point of libraries, we said, is that you must return what you borrow. The Deselit wanted to make amends. They went back to their starships which lay fuming on the horizon, and emerged days later with exact copies of the books they had devoured. Good as new.

The Deselit ambassador tried to explain. The shortest translation was something like "the teeth remember everything".

With the advent of datacube technology, physical books were mostly obsolete. We built new libraries that doubled as eateries for our alien friends. They regard ink on paper as a great delicacy, but only after the books have been in circulation for some time. They like the taste of our thumbprints, the bits of dried food, whatever unmentionable fluids cause pages to stick together. Making meals of a reader's creased history.

At first we tried filling the shelves with volumes of blank paper. But people had no reason to turn the pages, dogear the corners, break the spines. So we put interesting stories in them, so humans could prepare the books how the Deselit liked. They say this is the best way to understand us, so exotic a species, so far from the intimacies of home.

Sagan Yee is an animator and media artist who lives, works, and breathes (in that order) out of Toronto, Canada. At the time of this publication, they were probably making a videogame about ever-changing cityscapes and ridiculously long brunch lineups.

KITE-FIGHTING

K-MING CHANG

FeiFei is the one who teaches us flight. How to burn holes into the kite's skin with a cigarette butt so the wind threads through. FeiFei lights a cigarette, coats the string in powdered glass and rice glue. She takes us out to the abandoned lot behind the apartment building and shows us how to feed our kite to the mouth-sized sky. When I ask her if kites bleed, if they feel pain, she laughs and says not to worry: kites are too hollow for hurt. The point of fighting, she says, is to fly. To stay in the sky longer than shangdi. Keep the line taut so it cuts clean, she tells me. If it goes slack, the kite will sway. She steers the body of the kite like a blade. She told me once that our cousin caught his kite in a power line and got electrocuted when he tried to tug it down. That's why we don't have electricity sometimes, she said. Because his ghost forbids the light from fondling our bones. The thing you need to learn, she tells me, is how to lose. Sometimes, she says, it's necessary to cut your own kite loose. Sometimes a crow mistakes your kite for a mate and fucks it full of holes. Or sometimes the kite coasts like smoke into a tree and you have to sever it clean. Every night when I call my mother in another country, when she tells me it'll be soon, soon she'll send for me, I tell her about the kites, FeiFei's next fight, how one day I'll open my window and the sky will release a new species, flocks and flocks of kites in every color, and I will reach out and snip each one free, send them all to California. I tell her to keep watch, wait. Someday the kites will gather above the salon where she works all day with six pairs of scissors and so many strangers. They will come, I say. They will carry the sky to you.

K-Ming Chang is a Kundiman fellow, a Lambda Literary Award finalist, and a National Book Foundation 5 Under 35 honoree. She is the author of *Bestiary* (One World/Random House, 2020) and the short story collection *Gods of Want* (forthcoming July 2022).

INTERVIEWS

INTERVIEW WITH ERIC SCOT TRYON BY AUDRA KERR BROWN

FLASH FROG

Congratulations on having four stories from Flash Frog selected for Best Microfiction 2022! What makes this even more amazing is that it's your first year as a literary magazine! What is it about Flash Frog that has made it such a success?

Thank you! I am still in a bit of shock from it all, and so grateful to Best Microfiction and Guest Judge Tania Hershman. When I think about how our first year exceeded all my expectations, I can only attribute that to the incredible flash community, to which I am also grateful. The flash community—especially on Twitter—is such a close group and such a supportive group, and they really embraced *Flash Frog* right from the outset! This led to a lot of submissions right away, and a lot of quality submissions. It may sound corny, but without the incredible writers who trust us with their work, we are just an empty website with some photos of cute frogs.

I think what has also helped is that I did not start

Flash Frog on a whim. Instead, I obsessively thought about it for six to eight months before actually going forward, and I'm thankful that I did. It helped me establish a really clear vision for the magazine.

In your estimation, what makes for a great micro? Is it the uniqueness of the story itself, or is it something/s more?

This is such a difficult question, as there's certainly not one right answer, and I also think my answer to this question is constantly evolving. But I guess to try and tackle it, we have to start with a micro's size, after all that's what it is named after. And in a story that is 400 words or fewer, every line, every *word* matters. A lot. There is no room for throwaways, no lazy sentences, or lines used to "set up" the story. A micro is not just about getting us from point A to point B. It matters *how* we get there. So I'm really drawn to stories that pay just as much attention to language and rhythm and pacing as they do to character and plot. Sentences that beg to be read aloud. Another great thing that happens in a strong micro when the writer is paying close attention to each line and word, is there is such a palpable *immediacy* to the piece that you don't always find in other mediums, a grabbing hold of the reader and not letting go. Lastly, I think it's important to mention that in a great micro, the reader is in charge of doing a lot of work. And in that way the piece becomes interactive. And to excel at this, I always say that what you leave out of a micro is just as important as what you put in. But of course the balancing of this can be like a high-wire act, which is why despite its size, writing a great micro is no easy task!

And so what I love about flash and micros is that when all of the above is done well *and* there's a unique story to tell, we are left with something so much bigger than the few hundred words. The impact and emotion can radiate and linger long after the final punctuation.

Can you list some mistakes, craft-wise, that would reduce a story's chance of being published in Flash Frog?

Well first off, I don't think of them as "mistakes." Some stories are just not a good fit for some magazines. I've seen stories we've passed on go on to publish in big journals and win awards. And I still don't regret passing on them. They weren't right for *Flash Frog*. And I get so excited seeing them find perfect a home somewhere else!

But I will say however, there does seem to be a certain type of story that we pass on most often. And they're what I call "and then" stories. These are pieces that try to fit a traditional short story into the size of a flash. And to do that, a writer will generally have to either speed up the story or thin it out, and to me the story feels like I'm reading *and then this happened and then this and then and then...* and then the story's over and yes, we've covered a lot of ground, but I don't feel I know anything about the characters or what they want or how they feel or how they might have changed. And there isn't time for those lines so lyrical and new that I want to reread them aloud over and over just to taste them on my tongue. And I think these stories happen when authors have the mindset that a flash story is just a shorter short story. And I don't think that's the case. Flash and micros are a medium unto themselves. So instead of trying to squeeze a 5,000 word story into a 500 word pair of pants, I'd rather the story adjust the scope, zoom in, and show us the gritty details of something much smaller in scale but bigger in resonance.

How does a typical issue come together? What's your process?

Well, we don't have traditional "issues" per se. We publish one story a week, every Monday. I chose Monday because what better way to start the week than by reading a great flash story, right?! As for my process... first of all, I'm a one-man show. It's just me at *Flash Frog*. So I'm constantly—daily—reading stories from the queue. And stories that grab my interest in some way get set aside for another read on another day. And then about once a week or so, I will reread all the stories I have set aside. And ones that I'm still excited about, I set them aside again. The process happens a couple times to the point where when I am ready to accept a story, I have already read it at least three to four, maybe five times, and all on different days (because our moods and perspectives are constantly changing and I don't want to be prisoner of the moment), and I've read the story out loud at least once as well. So after a handful of readings and hearing it out loud, if I'm still really excited about it, I know there's something special here.

On the "production" side of things: we also commission artists to create original works of art for each and every story. Artists are always reaching out to me, or me to them, and those I think would be a good fit sign up for pub dates far in advance. Then one month prior to that pub date, I will send the artist their story which gives them four weeks to create something original for that piece. During that month, I will also go back and forth with the author with any suggested edits I might have. Coordinating the art side of things definitely adds a lot more work to the magazine, but that collaboration, having original art, is really important to me and it's an aspect of *Flash Frog* I'm really excited about!

What does the future look like for Flash Frog?

I don't think I could talk about the future of *Flash Frog* without talking about the future of flash fiction as a whole. I love seeing where flash and micro-fiction are going as a genre. While I'm not new to writing or editing, I am relatively new to the world of flash, micros, and online lit mags. And even in my short couple of years, it's been incredible to see how it's grown, how it's starting to be taken more seriously. We're starting to see more flash festivals, flash panels, flash anthologies, etc. But I think, and I hope, that we're only just beginning. Flash is not a cute little mini version of short stories. It's a craft and a skill and a medium unto itself. And it has a readership and a community all unto itself as well. I truly believe that flash can do things that other mediums can't. And as more people are exposed to good flash, it will only continue to grow in prominence. And I'm excited for *Flash Frog* to be a big part of that!

What do you want writers to know before they submit to Flash Frog?

I guess I would want them to know how passionate I am about stories and the craft and this magazine. That I read each and every submission with interest. And while professionalism goes a long way, I'm also not the type of editor that cares if there's a typo in paragraph two or if my name is spelled wrong (as often happens) or if the story is single or double-spaced, or if you use Times New Roman or Garamond. I care about the words and the characters and the emotion created. Oftentimes, when working with a writer on a story we've accepted, we will go back and forth several times on a single line or even a single word, until we get it just right. And I *love* that! It's such a thrill for me to work with a talented writer on those sentence-level details. In flash—and especially in micros—every word matters! And lastly, I know it may sound clichéd, but I mean it when I say that we have to pass on a lot of good stories. And I hope writers remember that when we pass on their work. After all, there are only so many Mondays in a year!

INTERVIEW WITH BENJAMIN WOODARD AND CATHY ULRICH BY AUDRA KERR BROWN

ATLAS AND ALICE

Congratulations! Three pieces from Atlas and Alice are included in this year's Best Microfiction. In your estimation, what makes for a great micro? Is it the uniqueness of the story itself, or is it something/s more?

Benjamin Woodard: Uniqueness certainly draws in a reader. An unusual setting or perspective can separate one piece from the pack. But in my opinion, and as a microfiction writer myself, attention to language makes the most difference. Microfiction mirrors poetry in that way. A beautiful turn of phrase holds so much weight in a tiny story, and it's this level of craft that gives the best of microfiction its lingering hold over a reader.

Can you list some mistakes, craft-wise, that would reduce a story's chance of being published at Atlas and Alice?

Cathy Ulrich: The biggest (and most common)

mistake I come across in submissions is something I've seen called "throat-clearing," where the story kind of revs its engine for a few paragraphs before actually starting. It could be the story giving background information that isn't particularly necessary, it could be opening with description that bogs the action down.

For me, I want to get right into the meat of the story from the get-go. Tight, taut prose is just so lovely! It's essential in micros, but it's wonderful to see in longer stories as well.

BW: I completely agree with Cathy here. If you're working with 400 words, you can't wait too long to leap into the narrative. Figure out the pivot point of your story, find the first piece of action that leads to that pivot, and start from there.

Next year Atlas and Alice will be celebrating its 10th anniversary! Kudos! Since your debut in 2013, many literary magazines have, unfortunately, come and gone. In addition to publishing some of the greatest writing on the internet, what has been your formula for success?

BW: It's funny, when the magazine started, I was a fiction editor, but after our first issue, I suddenly became the leader, and I had no idea what I was doing. That version of me would have laughed at the thought of *A+A* making it a decade. But here we are, and I think part of the reason we're still around has to do with our small masthead, our flexibility, and our general ethos of "let's do this because it is fun." Nobody is being paid, so if we're not enjoying the experience, the work becomes a chore, and once that happens, it's easy for a publication to go south.

We don't have a strict publishing schedule. We open submissions when we as editors have time to work. Some years, we put out three issues. Other years, we put out two (though they are usually massive in length). In that way, we work when the time feels right, rather than forcing ourselves into frustrating scenarios.

Have you been seeing an increase of microfiction in your submissions queue? If so, to what do you attribute this growth?

CU: We have! When I first started reading for *Atlas and Alice*, we definitely received more long submissions than flash, and it was pretty rare to see microfiction in the queue. We still get a lot of longer pieces (and we love them!), but there's definitely a lot more micros popping up in our submissions.

I think the form is growing as more and more writers become familiar with it and get more comfortable working with it. Making it their own. What I love about microfiction is how there are so many things it can be—it's such a joy seeing what different writers create.

Do you think we are experiencing the so-called "golden years" of microfiction? Where do you think the form is headed?

BW: I hope we're in a golden age. I suppose it's hard to know until the time has come and gone and we look back. For years, I've been arguing that flash and micro should be more popular. As creatures, we're always so busy, and a story that takes a minute or two to read should be a perfect escape. Though the pandemic may have slowed us all a bit, we still need these tiny journeys to get through the day, and in a perfect world, over the next year or two, more and more microfiction collections will appear on bookstore shelves.

Your tagline is "a magazine of intersections." What makes a story perfect for Atlas and Alice?

BW: When we started *Atlas and Alice*, we leaned toward a combination of science and art, but over time, the idea of intersection has evolved. Sometimes, a piece publishes as fiction, yet it could double as a prose poem. Sometimes, a piece mixes styles, or techniques, midstream. But an intersection can also be much simpler: real and fantastic, serious and funny. A perfect story is going to see the world for what it is: a three-dimensional space full of gray areas, full of contradictions, where opposing emotions can coexist and play with each other.

THREE ESSAYS ON THE CRAFT OF MICROFICTION BY PEOPLE WHO KNOW WHAT THEY'RE TALKING ABOUT

THEORIES OF LINGUISTICALLY ORIENTED MICROFICTION AND THE ROLE OF THE AUTHOR AS STORYTELLER, CHARLATAN, AND SEEKER IN A CRUEL AND GODLESS WORLD

SOREN COURT, FOUNDER OF THE FLASH FICTION COLLECTIVE

Theory no. 1: Language is a tool of precision. Words can accurately represent the world. The author (as in one who has authority) presents a world with their words like God from Genesis. A story is told. People revere the author. The author gets paid.

Theory no. 2: Language is a tool of imprecision. Words inherently fail to accurately represent the world. The author (as in a person who imagines themselves to be a person of authority, but who is really a mystical waif in an immense and cold universe) evokes a world with telling hints, evocative images, whorls of suspense, fleeting glimpses, subtextually-oriented language, attempts at the sublime, and a whole lot of back story that is never revealed.

In other words, if all language is errant translation of an already blurry world, fewer words might offer *less errancy*. Or less is more as a lesser intelligence once posited.

So the author isn't God, but the Easter Bunny.

The author is the Easter Bunny as tarot card reader, divining the story, and telling it with hidden eggs. The author is the Easter Bunny as tarot card reader who almost never gets paid and certainly gets no respect.

My invoice is in the mail and I accept PayPal.

TRUTH AS THE VEHICLE TO TRUTH

EMMANUELLE DICKINSON

Tell all the truth, but tell it slant*

Tell all the truth, but tell it _____

Tell all the truth.

Tell it slant.

Tell

It

{ }

* The truth God has served us in this world cannot be perceived by direct means.

HOW TO READ AND WRITE TINY THINGS

BOB EINSTEIN

It's called microfiction.

As in a story that needs a different lens to be seen.

Not reading glasses. Not a magnifying glass. A microscope.

It looks easy, but it's not (funny how people think small things are less significant than big things, how they're less in all ways).

You place your story on a slide. You look through the eyepieces of the microscope and move the focus knob until the image comes into focus. You adjust the distance between the eyepieces until you can see the story clearly with both eyes simultaneously (you should see the story in 3D).

Now, hold it—this is the moment most people mess up. Most people look quickly at the story and move on. Sure, you can see it all in a single glance, but you can't see it all in a single glance (imagine Yoda saying that sentence and reread it). You have to pause and notice. You have to pause and study. Take notes. Pause again. Repeat this many times.

Sometimes as many as 47 times.

To see a story in this way is a miracle. The way you get to see the thin line of a cell membrane. The way you get to see worlds within worlds. Protozoa. Phytoplankton. The shape of a cell, its nucleus, mitochondria.

If you've never looked at a story in this way, practice by looking at ordinary things under a microscope. You see alien lands. "Alien," as in belonging to or constituting another place or person. Try it with your hand. That hand on your arm. Especially if you have hairy hands. Or even if you have hands with just skin on them.

You become alien. You realize the world is alien. God is alien. Your mother is probably alien.

And this is the gift of microfiction: you get to see the alien side of what most people see as an ordinary universe. You get to see the small things that make everything work.

And you don't really need a microscope. I was just using that as a metaphor.

BEST MICROFICTION THANKS THE JOURNALS WHERE THESE PIECES APPEARED IN 2022.

"Calling at: Pharmacy, Florist, and Off-Licence only" by Lucy Goldring from *100 Word Story*.

"The Dragon and It" by Kate Francia and "The Taste of Our Pages" by Sagan Yee from *Apex Magazine*.

"Unfading" by Nathalie Handal from *Aster(ix)*.

"Alice, Some of the Time" by Abbie Barker, "Underage." by Jessica June Rowe, and "A Tragic Misstep in Evolution" by Marvin Shackelford from *Atlas and Alice*.

"Romance in the lower and upper atmosphere" by Frankie McMillan from *Atticus Review*.

"Giver of Gifts" by Jeff Friedman from *B O D Y*.

"Chicken-Girls and Chicken-Ladies and All the Possibilities of Pillowcases" by Exodus Oktavia Brownlow from *Barren Magazine*.

"Chicken Dinner" by Morgan Bennett from *beestung*.

"Ten Amazing Facts About the Human Body" by Joanna Theiss and "Writer's Jeopardy" by Paul Beckman from *Bending Genres*.

"Lightweight" by Brett Biebel and "Shy, Solitary Animals" by Kristin Bonilla from *Cease, Cows*.

"Contingencies" by Susan Perabo from *CRAFT*.

"Going Down" by Tim Craig from *Ellipsis Zine*.

"Jump" by Andrea Lynn Koohi from *Emerge Literary Journal*.

"Iron Hans" by Julie Cadman-Kim from *Fairy Tale Review*.

"Taking Turns" by Frankie McMillan from *Flash Boulevard*.

"All the Things They Couldn't Hand Back" by Emma Phillips from *Flash Fiction Magazine*.

"After the Thrill" by Amy Lyons, "Tokyo Pearl" by Teresa Plana, "Allsorts" by Sarah Salway, and "I Do Not Want to Live Without You" by Cathy Ulrich from *Flash Frog*.

"Same Old (notes to self)" by Janean Cherkun from *Flash Frontier*.

"Cords" by Isabelle B.L and "Tapeworm" by Kristen Loesch from *FlashBack Fiction*.

"Riding a Bike Without Training Wheels" by Jennifer Todhunter from *Ghost Parachute*.

"A Girl Makes Lemonade" by Ruth Joffre from *HAD*.

"Kite-Fighting" by K-Ming Chang from *Hayden's Ferry Review.*

"Swamp Thing Explains How Time Passes in the Middle of Dueling Crises" by Jack B. Bedell and "None of Us" by Becca Yenser from *Heavy Feather Review.*

"You Will Never Need to Walk Again" by Yunya Yang from *Janus Literary.*

"It was 1687 when an apple fell in natural motion" by Tanya Castro from *Lost Balloon.*

"Bowerbird" by Gabrielle Griffis, "Don't Get Lost in the Dinosaur Kingdom" by Cortney Phillips Meriwether, and "Let's" by L Mari Harris from *matchbook.*

"Girl as Music Box Ballerina" by L Mari Harris from *Milk Candy Review.*

"Mother-Daughter" by Kathryn Kulpa, "Bitter Hot Chocolate" by Sudha Balagopal, and "Excavating" by Aleyna Rentz from *Monkeybicycle.*

"Wobble" by Peter Anderson and "Canvas" by Scott Garson from *MoonPark Review.*

"Codes to Live By" by Jude Higgins from *New Flash Fiction Review.*

"The Historian" by Andrew Bertaina , "In the Town Where All the Final Girls Live" by Meghan Phillips, and "What I Think King Kong Is About (Having Never Seen King Kong)" by Kirsten Reneau from *No Contact.*

"Where There's Smoke" by Leslie Walker Trahan from *Okay Donkey*.

"history lesson" by Jenzo DuQue and "The woman who cuts my hair says she's been hearing noises in her apartment" by Leslie Walker Trahan from *Passages North*.

"Fridays" by Jennifer Todhunter and "Salvage" by Lacey Yong from *perhappened*.

"The Flood" by Matt Barrett and "Your Life as a Bottle" by Sarah Freligh from *Pithead Chapel*.

"What Grief Is" by Kinneson Lalor from *Reflex Fiction*.

"Calla Lilies" by Tara Isabel Zambrano from *Salt Hill*.

"Inheritance" by Grace Q. Song from *SmokeLong Quarterly*.

"Chickens in the Parlor" by Robert Scotellaro from *South Florida Poetry Journal*.

"Sea Monsters" by Susan Triemert from *Splonk*.

"She Has Lost Something Again" by Melissa Llanes Brownlee from *The Birdseed*.

"Her Kingdom Come" by Kristen Zory King, "Freezing Point" by Star Su, and "Left to their own devices they became them" by Michelle Morouse from *The Citron Review*.

"Star Swallowed" by Olivia Wolford from *The Ekphrastic Review*.

"Rust Belt Triptych" by Lauren Kardos from *The Lumiere Review*.